S. W. Zeller

Biography of the Zeller Family

Emigration to America from Switzerland in the Year 1740 A. D

S. W. Zeller

Biography of the Zeller Family
Emigration to America from Switzerland in the Year 1740 A. D

ISBN/EAN: 9783337183226

Printed in Europe, USA, Canada, Australia, Japan

Cover: Foto ©Raphael Reischuk / pixelio.de

More available books at **www.hansebooks.com**

BIOGRAPHY OF THE

ZELLER FAMILY.

EMIGRATION TO AMERICA FROM SWITZER-
LAND, IN THE YEAR A. D. 1740.

———◆◆◆◆———

A SKETCH OF

THE KUMLER FAMILY,

AND INCIDENTS IN THE

Life and Travels of the Author.

S. W. ZELLER.

———

S. D. MAKEPEACE, PRINTER:
1893.

INTRODUCTION.

The Zeller and Kumler families were Germans. Both were originally from Switzerland; a hardy race of people, and both were of high moral and religious character. Both Grandfather Kumler and Grandfather Zeller's brother were Bishops in the United Brethren church. The latter had nine children—four boys and five girls; the former had eleven—seven boys and four girls. These families did a great deal towards founding the United Brethren church.

Bishop Zeller assisted in forming the first Annual Conference in Ohio. He emigrated to the state in 1805. Kumler emigrated in 1819, and located in the northern part of Butler county, while the former located about twenty miles farther north, in Montgomey county.

These families were remarkable for longevity as well as piety.

The writer, who is a grandson of the one, and also of the brother of the other Bishop, an l wishing to leave a few things on record to per petuate the names of these two worthy families. and also to leave on record some of the inci dents and events that occurred in his own life, is the only apology he has to make for writing this little book.

And if the literary minded are not inter-ested in reading it, it is nevertheless to be hoped, and it is the desire of the writer that the less cultivated and the less spiritual will be in duced to strive for a better life.

S. W. ZELLER.

Switzerland is located in the southwestern part of Europe, with Germany on the north, Austria on the east, the Mediteranean sea on the south and France on the west. It was settled in an early time by a hardy race of Germans. The early history of this country in its struggle for freedom has interested, and even excited the sympathies of the reader of history.

It was from this country that the ancestors of the Zeller family descended. We can trace the history of the family back to the great-grandfather, who came with his parents to America in the year seventeen hundred and forty, when a boy of eight years of age, and settled in Berks county, Pa., on a little stream called Sweet-arrow.

This great-grandfather of whom I speak

married in Pennsylvania and raised a family of
six boys. I cannot now tell you anything about
the girls, if there were an equal number or none
at all. Five of these six boys emigrated to Ohio
in 1805; three of them, namely, Adam, Andrew
and Henry, located in Montgomery county, ten
miles south of Dayton. The other two, Jacob
and John, settled in Hocking county, four miles
north of Logan. The latter was my grandfather, and although I have often been at his
grave, which is in a beautiful churchyard, where
the United Brethren have a flourishing society
near the county seat, I have no recollection of
ever seeing him.

My great-grandfather was in the prime of
life during the revolutionary war, being twenty-
four years of age at the time of the declaration
of independence. Whether he fought in the
war or not, and was noted for his bravery, I
am not able to say; but one thing is known,
the ancestors were a hardy race of people, and
temperate and industrious in their habits. It
is said "every family has its black sheep;" but
this is not always true. I am truly glad that
the blood of my ancestors was free from the
taint of intoxicating liquor. I believe this is

of this very prevalent drink. Andrew and Jacob, became ministers in the U. B. church, about the year 1790. Andrew assisted in organizing the first Conference in Ohio, in the year 1809, and served honorably, as Presiding Elder, for a number of years; and he was elected a delegate to the first General Conference, in the year 1815, when he was elected Bishop, which office he filled with acceptability, for a period of six years. John Lawrence says of him, in church history, "His good sense, deep piety, and liberality, contributed greatly to the prosperity of the cause of Christ, especially in the Miami valley, where his influence will be perpetuated to the end of time."

Bishop Zeller, as he appeared at four score, is described as a little above the medium hight, and remarkably straight; hair white and on the top of his head, thin; eyes gray and full, and skin very fair. To the last year of his life he walked perfectly erect and with a quick and measured step. He was the father of nine children, who occupied such an important relation to the church in Ohio, and a large number of their descendants are now active workers in the church, in the Miami Valley, is the only apology for giving the names of the children of Bishop Zeller. They are as follows: John, Andrew, George, Michael, Catherine, Elizabeth, Barbery, Christena and Mary. Four of the latter were companions of noted ministers of the U. B. church, namely, Bishop H. Kumler, Jacob Antrim, John Kemp and Henry Evinger. The latter's remains lie in Otterbein cemetery, in Hutton township, Coles Co., Ill. Bishop Zeller died May 25, 1839, in the 84th year of his age.

Adam, the Bishop's brother, was married twice and had two children by his first wife and three by his last wife.

Henry, another brother, died without issue.

Jacob, another brother, had three children born to him. I have knowledge of two of the girls and one boy; the former married Raudabaugh, and Matthias. The Raudabaugh family still lives four miles north of Lancaster, and Matthias near Logan. Isaac and Jacob Matthias and their sister Stivison, grandchildren of Jacob, were active christians.

John, still another brother and the writer's grandfather, had five children, namely, Benjamin, John, Jacob, Peter and Mary. The latter married Judge Pullen of Logan, Ohio. Judge Pullen was a good, intelligent man and exerted quite an influence in Hocking county. He was accidently killed at a house raising in the city of Logan. The Judge had by Mary his wife, five children; two boys and three girls. These raised respectable families. Three of these families lived in the vicinity of where I preached three years, namely, 1868–69–70—and with whom I became intimately acquainted. A son of the Judge was the leading physician of the city of Logan at the time alluded to. His sister was the wife of Moses Fry, who was also a physician, living two miles from the city, and was an active member of the Baptist church. The families of the other two children moved somewhere to the west and it was not my privilege to form an acquaintance with them.

Benjamin Zeller, father's oldest brother, was a minister of the Evangelical association. He was a good man, but in his old age was very poor as far as this world is concerned. He sold a small farm near Logan, Ohio, about 1857 and emigrated to Illinois; there he invested his money in another farm which was incumbered with mortgage, and lost everything he had.

Jacob and Peter were the youngest of the family. Both of them learned the carpenter trade with father. The latter favored father very much with the exception of being less in stature. The former was quite corpulent, a good specimen of the Swiss German. He raised a large family and his oldest son, very much the build of his father, had one still more numerous. These two uncles and the other members of their families were members of the M. E church and influential citizens.

My father, John Zeller, was a man six feet in hight, rather slim built, with black eyes and dark complexion. In several particulars he was an exception to the rest of the connection, who were rather corpulent, with blue eyes and fair complexion. He was born in Berks county, Pa, in the fall of 1797 and emigrated with his parents to Lancaster, Fairfield county, Ohio, where they remained for a few months only. During the winter of this year the family were annoyed by some one stealing their hay. Grandfather remarked one day that their hay was going very rapidly, he feared some one was taking it. Benjamin, the oldest of the boys, replied that he would look after the matter, which he did quite successfully. He hid himself near the hay one dark night to await further developments. After waiting awhile, he heard the light footsteps of some one coming, who secured a good bundle of hay, got it on his back and started off. Uncle slipped up behind the thief with a dark lantern and set fire to the hay. Soon it was ablaze. The thief dropped the hay and ran off terribly frightened. Not knowing where the fire came from, he probably thought it was a judgment from heaven sent upon him. This was the last hay that was taken. This circumstance was related to me by my uncle himself when he was an old man, and there were old persons who remembered something of the occurrence, when I lived in Lancaster more than fifty years after it happened.

In the spring of 1815 father left the place of his youthful days spent along the Hocking river and came west to Montgomery county, about ten miles south of Dayton, Ohio, and made his home with the Rev. Henry Evinger, who had married his cousin, Andrew Zeller's daughter. Here he was an apprentice three years with his cousin and cousin by marriage, where he learned the carpenter trade. After he had completed the time of his apprenticeship he continued to labor with his boss, as a journeyman, three years more. During the early period of his stay with Rev. Evinger he embraced religion and joined the United Brethren church, in which he was a consistent and faithful member. Sometime during these six years, not far perhaps from the time he finished his trade, he was licensed to preach the gospel and joined the Miami annual conference.

In the fall of 1821 he was joined in marriage with Susanna Kumler, daughter of Bishop H. Kumler, who resided near Mintonville, Butler county, Ohio. Soon after his marriage he settled on a farm lying within and near the forks of two streams—Seven Mile and Four Mile—being somewhat nearer the latter. This farm was located about six miles north of Hamilton, the county seat of Butler county, Ohio. Here father made his home from 1821 to 1830. During this time four children were born; three boys and one girl. Father rented his farm and worked at the carpenter trade. During these nine years he did a large amount of hard work.

There are a number of houses and barns he built in Butler county, O., three quarters of a century ago, still standing as monuments of his industry and skill. A large part of the work, he performed between the years 1817 and 1840, during which time he instructed a number of men in the same art. Not far from the summer of 1833 he did the carpenter work of a large brick Presbyterian church—40 by 60 feet, with a self-supporting roof. There was more timber used in that roof than there is now used in building four roofs of the same size. This was considered wonderful skill in those days.

He was also an active worker as a local preacher. His sabbaths were usually employed in preaching in destitute neighborhoods. After working hard all week he would often ride twelve or fifteen miles and preach for the people. From 1844 to 1850 a large part of his time was spent in the ministry. Sometimes he would preach for the English people and sometimes for the German. He preached a great many funerals and solemnized many marriages.

After his marriage he first settled on a

farm one mile and a half southwest of where there is now a beautiful village called Seven Mile. This village is located six miles north of Hamilton, the county seat of Butler county. Here he resided from 1821 to the spring of 1830, at which time he moved on a farm west of Hamilton six miles. Here is where he lived the rest of his days.

Father was a progressive man, and in the front rank with the reformers of his time. He zealously advocated the cause of temperance; and he did this by example as well as precept. I never knew him to use intoxicating liquor. I heard him relate rather an amusing incident which occurred soon after he was married: His brother-in-law, Jacob Flickinger, lived near by and ran a distillery. He was father's senior about twenty years, and had been twice married. Father thought his experience in house-keeping, therefore, would be of immense value to a young man just commencing. Flick-inger said to Father one day that he ought to get a barrel of whisky as he was commencing house-keeping. Father took his advice, and succeeded in getting it safely in the cellar. But as time rolled on he found it an article altogether useless to him, only as it was occasionally needed for sickness. It lay in his cellar for years until it became noted as the oldest, and therefore the best liquor that could be obtained in cases of sickness, and persons would come from far and near and get it for invalids. In this way father succeeded in disposing of his liquor, and after this it was one of the scarce commodities of the family.

I remember when a small boy it was used in the harvest field and at house and barn raisings, but I never knew father to taste it; he said he could not not use it at all. I remember, as far back as 1835, he and a few others would not use any liquor, even for harvest times, and he furnished those with tobacco who would not use whisky. He was among the early anti-slavery reformers, and about the year 1847, he withdrew from the Democratic party, which had kept him in office almost continually in the township, and identified himself with the Liberty party. For some time he and two neighbors met at the polls and voted their sentiments on this subject.

He died after protracted illness and severe suffering from kidney affliction in the fall
of 1857, just about the time he completed his
three score years.

THE KUMLER FAMILY.

My grandfather on mother's side of the house, was Bishop Henry Kumler, Sr. His ancestors were from Switzerland, also. They are of German origin, descended entirely from German ancestors. Grandfather Kumler was born in Pennsylvania, January 3, 1775. After passing the usual catechical course, he was received into the German reformed church, in Greencastle, Pa. In 1811 he was awakened to a sense of his sinful condition. In his youthful days God's spirit had often impressed him with the necessity of living a christian life, and he had as often resolved so to do; but his resolutions were not put into practice until he was about thirty-six years of age. He now felt that God had given him the last call, and that unless he accepted of Jesus Christ as his Savior he would be lost. His distress was great. He abandoned his work and sought a secret place to pray, and determined never to cease until he obtained mercy. He obtained the clear evidence of his acceptance with God while at prayer in his barn. He ran to the house and told his wife of the great salvation. That evening he held family worship for the first time. United Brethren preachers called on him and preached in his home. This, with the prayers and speaking in which he participated, excited the displeasure of his pastor, who one sabbath preached a sermon for his benefit; saying, those people who pray in public are Pharisees—they opened their windows so the people might hear them pray.

This hurt Kumler's feelings very much. Some of the cold, formal members were pleased with the discourse, and laughed, looking at him; and as the congregation retired one of this class hunched him and asked if he knew for whom the sermon was preached. Kumler wrote the pastor a letter saying he could get no sense out of the sermon; that the scriptures taught that christians should let their light shine, and not hide it under a bushel. When his pastor read the letter, he sent for Kumler, and as he entered the room he said:

" Never in your life undertake to write to a preacher again."

"Why not?"

"Because, when you only say a thing and find that you are cornered, then you can say, 'I did not mean so.'"

Kumler said, " What I have written I have written."

The pastor then said, drawing the letter from his pocket, "Well, come and sit down. What do you understand by letting your light shine?"

"To let my light shine, is to show by my life before God and man that I am living a better life," replied Kumler.

" Oh, that is well enough."

" And I believe that a man with a family should pray with and for them."

"That's well enough."

" Yes," continued Kumler, " God be praised, I feel happy in doing my duty toward my family and neighbors; and whosoever will may call it hypocrisy."

The pastor said he should not have preached the sermon, but not less than three came to him and said "You will lose Kumler." Thus ended the interview and also Mr. K.'s connection with the German Reformed church.

Mr. Kumler was licensed to preach, and received into the U. B. church at Hagerstown, Md., in 1813. In 1815 he was a delegate to the first general conference of the church. His first circuit required 370 miles travel every four weeks. In 1817 he was elected presiding elder. In 1819 he emigrated to Ohio, and settled in Butler county. In 1825 he was elected Bishop and re-elected in 1829, 1833, 1837, 1841. During the first eight years of his superintendency he crossed the Alleghanies by private conveyance eighteen times.

Bishop Kumler was neat and comely. His countenance was open and pleasant and he was possessed of much cheerfulness and great thought. His mind was well balanced and he was a grand leader in church matters.

MRS. HENRY KUMLER.

Grandmother Kumler's maiden name was Wengert. She was born in Pennsylvania October 1, 1779, and died November 30, 1874, being a little more than ninety-five years of age.

Hannah, her oldest child, was born October 12, 1798, and died February 5, 1892, being more than ninety-three years old.

Henry, the second child, was born January 10, 1801. He became an eminent minister in the U. B. church, and for several years, Bishop He died August 19, 1882, being over eighty years old.

Mother, Susanna, was born January 3, 1804, and died September 30, 1877, being nearly seventy-four years of age. I will speak of her again.

Elizabeth, the third girl, was born July 5, 1805. Her death occurred in 1878.

D. C., who was a successful physician, and the wittiest one of the family, was born September 30, 1807, and died November 8, 1881, being a little over seventy-four years of age. Luther, a son of his, is a Presbyterian minister.

Elias, the fifth in order, was born October 21, 1809, and died December 6, 1873, aged sixty-four. He was the best financier of all the children. A son of his is Dr. Kumler, of Pittsburg.

Jacob and Michael, twins, were born August 31, 1811. They are still living—the oldest twins in Ohio. Each have a son in the ministy.

Joseph was born February 23, 1813. He is still living.

John, the youngest boy, was born December 24, 1814, and died October 26, 1891. He left five boys who are lawyers and successful in business.

Catherine, the youngest of the family, was born April 6, 1817, and died August 11, 1889.

MRS. JOHN ZELLER.

I said I would write of mother again. Here it is:

Mother, in her looks and general character, was very much like her father; and without a doubt was one among the best women that ever lived. She was much interested in the moral culture and training of her children and was much gratified to believe they were striving to live good lives. After father's death mother took care of her mother (who lived to be almost ninety-six years old and was a great charge) for eighteen years, and spared no labor or sacrifice to make her comfortable in her declining years, and mother would probably have lived several years longer had she not taken the responsibility of this charge.

Mother lived about two years after grandmother's death, which time was spent with Catherine, her youngest daughter, who lived in the state of Indiana. She often said, in the last years of her life, "If it was the will of God she would like to be taken from this life suddenly, when she was no longer able to labor, so that she would not be a charge to others as her mother was." This demise was granted her even better than she had asked for. She appeared to have a premonition of her departure. She said to an invalid grandchild, in the morning of the day of her departure, "Oh, John, I wish I could take you with me to Heaven today." This was on Sabbath morning, the last day of September, 1877. Her daughter asked her to go with her to church a mile distant. "No," she replied, "I will stay at home and read the Bible." She did read the Bible and in addition to this prepared a good dinner for the family by the time they returned, and ate a hearty dinner. She then read the Bible again, afterward lying down to rest awhile, falling to sleep. Her daughter awoke her at lunch time when she arose and ate again for the last time. She took sick about eight o'clock, and in half an hour all was over and she had departed this life. Here are a few lines I wrote on the impulse of the moment when the news came of her death:

MY MOTHER. How interesting the name of mother is to us all. But my mother is no more—or rather, is gone to live with Jesus and the angels in the better land. On Sabbath night, as the last hours of the month of September were passing away, and while pleasantly associated with members of Lower Wabash Conference we were having a solemn and very impressive communion season, my dear mother way passing through the valley of the shadow of death, and by the time our communion service had ended she had also ended her earthly pilgrimage, and without doubt she is now realizing what it is to be with Jesus and enjoy the bliss of heaven.

Oh my mother! that you are now safe and happy at home, shall I meet you there? I shall never forget your sympathy and kindness to me when I was a little boy. Well do I remember when I was about eight years of age I was sick and you did so much to alleviate my pain. So, cheerfully did you deprive yourself of sleep and rest to administer to my comfort.

But after all, what interests me more than all besides, are the efforts you made for my spiritual welfare. I may not know how much I am indebted to you for your prayers and example and counsel until I meet you in that better land. Oh those memorable hours of my awakening. When sin became to me exceedingly sinful; your prayer in Jesus' name had access to the throne of grace, the gloom of condemnation passed away and the light of pardoning love came to my relief. Mother, rest on in that heavenly land, and, Jesus helping me, I will meet you by and by.

I will now give short sketches of the lives of my brothers and sisters: .

Daniel K. is the oldest of the family. He was born October 2, 1822. In build and disposition he is much like mother. He is a good, benevolent man. He was a successful farmer and labored hard until he was forty years of age. About this time he enlisted in defense of his country, and was chosen captain of a company of National Guards, in which capacity he served three months. About one year after he was mustered out of service, he left the farm and moved to Richmond, Ind., and bought out the city bakery, and has so conducted that business as to make considerable money.

Soon after he moved to Richmond, he took a letter from the U. B. church and joined the Presbyterian church; was at once ordained an elder in that church, which office he has filled with acceptability ever since. The most of the time he has held the office of city councilman, and was county commissioner, and took an active part in building the new court house.

Susanna, the oldest sister, was born November 11, 1828. She married David Zartman, and moved about the year 1857 to Carroll county, Ind., eleven miles south of Logansport. She raised a large family.

Jacob A. Zeller was born October 30, 1830. He graduated from Miami University; was a student in college with President Harrison and Whitelaw Reid. He has devoted his life to giving instruction in the high schools of Indiana.

His first efforts were made, however, in conducting the Union school of the city of Oxford, where he graduated. After spending several years here, his second charge was the High school of Evansville, Ind., where he remained in charge eleven years. He then took charge of all the city schools of Richmond, Ind., as Superintendent, where he remained for three years.

He is now in charge of the High school of Lafa ette, where he has been working nearly six years. He is widely known in Indiana as an educator. As an evidence of what the students think of him, after being their instructor for eleven years in the city of Evansville, the young men and ladies who received their education under him voluntarily made him a present of a gold watch and chain worth $125.

He was a soldier three months.

Elizabeth Zeller was born March 8, 1834. She married Jacob Schell. She had five children; all boys. She died November 7, 1864, aged nearly thirty-one years. She was the most deeply pious of our family. A short time before her death she had all her boys come to her bedside and put her hands on their heads and asked God's blessing on them, and said if it was the Lord's will she would like for them to be ministers of the Gospel of Jesus Christ. Four of them are now engaged in this calling.

Catherine Zeller was born April 20, 1837. She married Jacob Carr, by whom she had a large family. She died January 18, 1881.

Joseph S. Zeller was born August 1, 1841. He enlisted as a soldier at the commencement of the war, and came out as hearty and healthy as any one who served as long as he did.

Elias R. Zeller was born September 13, 1844. He enlisted in his country's service as a soldier and served three months. After the war, he entered Miami University and graduated. He then took charge of a Burlington, Iowa, paper as its editor, and supported Greeley. He resigned this position and took charge of the schools of Winterset, Iowa, where he labored for five years. He has been engaged as editor, and farmer alternately since.

Henry was born September 14, 1824, and died in February, 1840.

John Michael was born July 28, 1839, and died in February, 1840.

Grandfather Kumler's sister married Mr. Hibschman. She had by him four boys and four girls. Henry, John, Daniel, and Samuel; and the girls were Elizabeth, who married Fasic; Eva, married Winters; Catharine, married Strickler; Sarah, married Rev. Rupp, their son, Daniel, is also a minister, and their daughter married George Sando, who is also a minister. The three last named were ministers in the Church of God.

Then there is a generation of the Hibschmans, grandchildren of Grandfather Kumler's sister, who live mostly in Illinois, namely: Benjamin, John, Henry, Daniel, Samuel and Jacob; also, Sarah, Elizabeth, Katherine, Sophia and Malinda. The maiden names of the latter were Hibschman. Then there were quite a number of her grand-children that I am not able to speak of.

CHAPTER I.

It is remarkable how far back into the history of early life the active memory will take us. I remember incidents that occurred when I was not more than three years of age. I was born September 13, 1826, in sight of where there is now the beautiful village of Seven Mile, situated in the Miami valley, Butler county, Ohio, six miles north of Hamilton, the county seat. In the spring of 1830, when I was between three and four years of age, father moved to Hanover township, same county, on Indian creek, about six miles west of Hamilton. The circumstances attending this removal are as fresh in my memory as if they had only occurred last week. I will refer to one:

When we were ready to start, wagons all loaded, and the stock gathered together in the farm yard, all on tiptoe of excitement, as is the case usually with movers—boys of three years as anxious to be off as those of riper years. Just at this time the heavens gathered over with dark clouds portending a storm, and true to the omens of nature the rain descended, delaying the anxious trip an hour or two. Not unlike this does it often occur with us in our religious life. When we are about to engage in an important enterprise then the moral heavens gather in darkness, and discouragements meet us at every step in life.

Very early in life I was sensibly impressed with the sinfulness and depravity of my nature. The first act of wickedness of which I was guilty, that made a deep impression on my mind, was perpetrated when I was about six years of age. The circumstances connected with this sin are as follows:

Soon after father arrived at his new farm on Indian creek he, being a carpenter by trade, built a new dwelling house. The old house which stood near by was then occupied as a shop in which father worked in the winter

season, at the cabinet business. Father was
somewhat strict in his orders forbidding his
children to use his tools. One day when father was absent my oldest brother, who was four
years older than myself, went into the shop, and
being anxious to construct a toy which he im-
agined would be of immense value; the temptation being too great he transgressed father's
law. Now, about this time I found my way into
the shop. At once I said to brother, I will tell
father that you are using his tools. Brother
said, If you will not tell I will make you a nice
toy. Whether I consented to it I do not remember; but brother commenced making me
the toy at once. He labored until the sweat
ran down his face, then when the work was finished I took the toy and leaving the shop said,
I will tell on you, anyway.

But I did not long retain a cheerful heart;
that day was spent in gloom and unhappiness.
Although I did not inform father what occurred
still the pain I inflicted on brother was a
source of deep regret to me. For days the
scene would come up before me afresh; the
toil, anxiety and sweat of brother to complete
the toy, and then my base ingratitude after-

ward afflicted me deeply. Whether I made any concession or asked forgiveness I can not certainly say; as a number of years have passed since these things occurred.

Often during the next six years I was troubled on account of my sins. Sometimes after the troubles of the day were ended and when retired to bed for the night, I would be effected to tears for my life of impiety and irreligion. In the year of 1838 with my parents I attended a campmeeting on the banks of the Big Miami river, about ten miles from the mouth. Revs. Antrim, Stubbs, and others of the pioneers of the U. B. church were in attendance. I remember a circumstance that occurred with father Stubbs. He entered the stand one day and arose to preach, when a number of the rowdies gathered around the stand and cried out, "That man can't preach," so that the largest part of the congregation heard it. The venerable old preacher replied, "well I will try, and after I get through, if you think you can better it you can have the opportunity." He proceeded to address the people as if nothing had occurred, from the following words, "The weapons of our warfare are not carnal, but mighty through God to the pulling down of the strongholds."—2d cor. 10:4. He preached a powerful sermon in the demonstration of the spirit, which resulted in convicting sinners and comforting the saints.

At this meeting the power of God was manifested in the awakening and happy conversion of many souls. It was during this meeting that I became powerfully awakened, and felt impressed as I had never been before with the importance of being a christian. My convictions did not arise so much from a sense of external wickedness, as a want of conformity to Gods righteous law. I felt a very deep sense of my ingratitude to God, for his infinite love was exhibited to me in a thousand ways, while my love and gratitude toward him was so exceedingly small. The meeting having progressed triumphantly for about ten days, it broke up amid the shouts of new born souls. It was the custom at the breaking up of camp, for the preachers to head the column of procession, and all christians to fall in line and march around the tent inclosure, at the same time singing beautiful hymns, and then before parting, take each other by the hand and giving the affectionate farewell, being impressed with the fact that it would never be their privilege all to meet again in this world. Thus closed the meeting referred to above, without any effort on my part to become an active christian. And indeed it was not expected that one so young as I would become a christian. Good christian parents thought it better for their children to wait till they were grown up, before they became active in religion. Up to this time no one had encouraged me to be a practical christian. I have stated that my awakening was the result of internal wickedness of the heart, rather than external; this was not owing however to any innate purity that I was thus fortunate, but it may be referred to the restraining influence of grace and the good example and instructions of pious parents.

While I owe to my parents a monument of everlasting gratitude for the moral and religious influence they exerted upon my mind in early life, still I think they erred in thinking that children in early life had better not make a public profession of religion.

I was exceedingly mortified after joining the church and making a public effort to be

a christian, on communion occasion, when the
ordinance of the sacrament was being observed,
I too felt it my duty to commune, and when on
my way to the communion table was met by
my father who advised me not to commune. I
passed on and out of the house with a sad
heart.

I suppose that my father had an idea that I
was not a very good christian, which was too
true, although I was trying sincerely to live a
good life. It may have been because I was
quite young. I am more than ever convinced
that christian parents should not only instruct
their children in the principles of morality and
religion, but also to impress upon their minds
the importance of being practical christians in
early life. It is said of Timothy that "from a
child he knew the scriptures which are able to
make him wise unto salvation." "I love them
that love me and they that seek me early shall
find me." But leaving the meeting without
consecrating myself to the service of Christ,
still the impression upon my mind continued
with me, and soon after, there being an opportunity given, I went forward voluntarily and
joined the church.

I shall never forget the question asked by the minister: "Do you wish to live a christian life?" I said I did, and was received into the church. After this I was often found at the mercy seat seeking salvation. I desired the blessings of God's grace to be imparted to me, as I had witnessed it imparted to others at the altar of prayer, but from some cause this was denied me.

About this period in my struggles against sin my awakening became powerful and conviction pungent.

One night in the winter of 1840, after retiring, I became so distressed that I could not restrain myself longer, and my cries and sobs attracted the attention of mother, who came to my bed and asked what was wrong. I replied, I am so wicked a feel so badly. The family all got up and we had prayer meeting until about midnight, but no relief came to my mind. I continued to make use of the means of grace especially prayer, public and private.

I shall never forget my class leader J. Zinn, who was so much interested in my spiritual welfare. He would often call upon me to pray in public. And it was on one of these occasions when we had met at God's house expressly for prayer and on a beautiful Sabbath day, while praying as best I could, that light came into my heart. Here I first felt the comforting influence of God's grace in the heart. Indeed there was light and joy in my heart corresponding to the light and beauty of the Sabbath day without.

I have realized since however, in this poor heart of mine the truth of this beautiful sentiment of the wise man: "The path of the just is as the shining light that shineth more and more unto the perfect day." Had I have had the proper instructions I verily believe a large part of this anxiety and trouble would have been avoided.

In February of the same year father's family was severely afflicted with typhoid fever. My two older and youngest brothers were victims of this disease. My youngest and next to the oldest died within a few days of each other. This was a very sad time and effected me very much. To be deprived of the society of two brothers in so short a time, the one a year, and the other fifteen years of age, was a source of sadness never to be forgotten; but religion which affords comfort in the darkest hours of life, was a source of real comfort now. It said to the afflicted parents and children, as they looked upon the pale forms, of never to be forgotten remembrance, these loved ones shall live again in the better land, where the inhabitants never complain of sickness and where death shall never come.

CHAPTER II

There is one thing remarkable in father's family, six boys and three girls, all embraced religion and joined the U. B. church before they reached the age of sixteen years.

. I had an intense struggle of mind with reference to the work of the ministry. At the age of sixteen years I felt it to be my duty to engage in this blessed work. But then when I would think of the greatness of this work, and the responsibility that rested upon the minister of Jesus Christ, I would banish the thoughts from my mind, and resist these impressions made by the Holy Spirit, as I verily believe, and I would say of myself, Why think of such a thing? you never will be able to enter upon

the high and holy office of the Christian minis
try. I had a lofty and most sacred idea of the
greatness of this work. I associated with this
work the principles of Intelligence, Goodness
and Purity, and even the presence of the infinite Jehovah as being with the minister of the
gospel, and then I would feel that these being
so far beyond the possibility of attainment by
myself the conclusion to my mind was clear, I
could never be a minister of the pure and holy
gospel of Jesus.

These impressions that I ought to work for
Jesus ever and anon would intrude themselves
upon me, right in the midst of other pursuits
and projects of a worldly nature in which I was
engaged. And thus it was that the contest
went on from the time I was sixteen to twenty-
four years of age when, after more than ordinary struggles of mind, I consented to accept of
license to exhort, which was given me at a
quarterly meeting held in the town of Millville,
Butler county, Ohio, May 18, 1850. The services of this meeting were conducted by Elder
Kumler, jr., whose worthy name is signed to
my first license.

I will state a few things further in regard to the struggles of my mind before I decided to enter the ministry. When about twenty-three years of age I determined to enter upon some permanent business for life. For the two past years, after having completed the time of my minority under the parental roof with kind and loving parents, I had devoted partly to farming and partly to teaching school. Now I resolved to devote the rest of my life to the occupation of farming.

I selected for my companion, Mary G. Landis, and upon the 17th day of May, 1849, the marriage ceremony was performed by the Rev. Samuel Williams, of the old school Baptist church. We moved upon a farm. I commenced work with fair prospect of success. It was not until the summer of 1849 that my trouble became truly great and anxiety alarming with regard to my call to the ministry. The larger part of my wakeful hours were spent in serious meditation and prayer upon this subject. And the more I thought and prayed upon this subject, the more I was convinced that I was doing wrong in resisting God's call to this work. But many new difficulties were now in the way of my entering upon the work of the ministry.

I had bought a farm and having but little means to pay for it, gave my obligations to pay for it in the future. This financial difficulty looked to me to be insurmountable. But there was another difficulty that appeared to be even greater than this: What will your wife say about this? A few months ago the consent of only one was required, but now it will require the consent of two. Ah, thought I, Mary will never consent to my leaving home, and spending my life in the itinerant work of the church. Now this thought came forcibly to my mind; An active, faithful life as a layman in the church is all that is required of me. So I began to think in what way I could make myself useful. I thought this: I could employ part of the evenings and also other scraps of time to labor for the good of souls, and determined to go and see a neighbor that night and talk with him upon the interest of his soul.

After supper, without saying a word to my wife, I started off on my first missionary effort. Now, while walking along, I felt well. I have ascertained at last what my duty is; it is to be a faithful layman in the church. And as I went along the way I thought success would at-

tend the effort and good would be accomplished
I was soon at the house of my friend, and with
some difficulty I introduced the subject of religion.

My friend who I thought could be persuaded to be a christian, led out in the discussion of man's responsibility and moral agency,
assuming the former and denying the latter.
I contended that these were inseparable, and
if we were responsible beings and accountable
to God, then necessarily we must be moral
agents, for the one implied the other. This he
denied, and the discussion went on for an hour
and I bade him good night and went home. As
I was returning I felt terribly disappointed; I
thought it was a perfect failure and I had accomplished nothing, and it was a long time before
I made another effort as a missionary.

Not long after this my youngest brother
took seriously ill with congestion of the brain.
He was about six years of age, and being the
youngest of the family, was a favorite with us
all. He grew worse and worse until his life was
despaired of, and three physicians said he must
die. As I looked upon his lovely, innocent

form I sincerely desired that he might live, and I said while standing by his bedside and looking him in the face: "O Lord, if thou wilt restore him to health again I will take this as an evidence that it is thy will that I shall engage in the work of the ministry."

I returned to my home one mile and a half from father's home, thinking of the vow I had taken, that if the boy gets well I will make an effort to become a minister of Jesus. The next day we were sent for in great haste to go to father's, for it was thought the boy was dying. My wife and I went as soon as we could to see him alive for the last time, as we thought, and here we were gathered around the couch waiting for the last gasp to close the scenes with him on earth. How solemn was the occasion! Father and mother, brothers and sisters waiting at the very margin of the river of death. I think none of that group felt as I did. Ah! did not father and mother feel as deeply upon this sad hour as any other could feel? Yes, surely. But in my case there was this complex state of feeling. When I looked upon the boy my heart was melted with sympathy at the thought of his death; and then a thought quite different would steal across the mind: you will now be relieved from all anxiety and doubt with reference to your call to the ministry. For indeed I had an honest, anxious desire to know the will of God upon this subject, and I believe I can truthfully say that no one subject more intensely and completly ever absorbed my mird than this. And now that this perplexing question was to be decided, and my mind set at rest, after years of agitation and trouble, was a matter of no small importance.

But the boy after lingering for several hours, and the struggle going on between life and death, commenced slightly to recover, and soon was well and hearty. New the matter of deep solicitude was only partially settled and I had terrible doubts if it was my duty after all to be a minister of Jesus and, like Gideon, wanted the Lord to give me still another sign. And so it is, we are slow to believe even when the Lord gives us clear evidence of his will concerning us.

Now, soon after this there was a precious revival of religion in the neighborhood and my companion, who had not up to this time professed faith in Jesus, became very much interested in the welfare of her soul, and as she presented herself at the altar of prayer I, desiring another evidence of my call to the ministry, said again to the Lord: If thou wilt convert my companion this night I will take this as the conclusive evidence that it is thy will that I should engage in the work of the ministry. She was converted that night, and I have been endeavoring ever since, though unworthily, to proclaim the precious words of salvation to the people.

I have already stated that at the age of twenty-four years I received license to exhort. At the close of the first year, the class to which I belonged recommended me to the quarterly conference for license to preach. H. Kumler was continued in the office of presiding elder, and after examination by the elder, the conference granted me license to preach the gospel. Whenever opportunity afforded, I at least made the effort to talk for Jesus, though it was in great weakness. Sometimes I realized great peace and comfort in the discharge of duty, and at other times there was impenetrable darkness and I would be greatly discouraged and feared

I should not succeed, and so it was for some time, a life of alternate sunshine and shadow. The Lord however blessed me with sustaining grace.

After sustaining a quarterly conference relation for one year I was recommended for membership in the Miami annual conference. The conference held its session this year at Pleasant Ridge chapel, Butler county, Ohio, about 3 miles west of Middletown. My license bears date September 4, 1852, signed by Bro. J. J. Glosbrenner, Bishop. I gave my name to the station committee for a field of labor. I was appointed to the Germantown circuit with J. W. Cochran, who had charge of the work.

We had a pleasant time together during the fall and winter. We were blessed with some good revivals of religion and my soul was happy in the Lord. It was not long however, until a dark cloud came down on the circuit and many hearts were made sad. A serious charge of immorality was made against the preacher in charge of the circuit. I thought these dark clouds of adversity would soon be driven away, and prosperity would again attend us, but I was sadly disappointed. J. W. Cochran resigned the work and arrangements were made by the presiding elder to investigate the case. I thought my colleague would be able to vindicate his character and prove his innocence. I felt a deep interest in this investigation and accompanied the presiding elder to Darke county, the place where my colleague lived and where the crime should have been committed. Darke county, Ohio. Rather significant, indeed before we were through with the investigation of the case, I thought truly, it is terribly dark here just now. But what was a source of unpleasantness to me, I was chosen as the third person to sit as juryman, and to assist in deciding this matter of my colleague. I objected of course, but being urged both by J. W. C. and the two other committeemen, I accepted, and the trial commenced.

I did my best to note all the evidence for and against my friend, for I felt I had a heavy responsibility upon me, and I desired to be prepared to do right. The evidence was very clear and decided against the poor man. And after a weary day was spent in the investigation of the evidence and half of the night hearing the pleadings of the attorneys, the case was submitted to us for decision. And now a move was made by the oldest member of the committee, that I thought was a little hard. Said he to, me, "You are the youngest member of the committee and therefore must give your verdict first." I could see but little logic in this, but as I might have been influenced by the decision of others, it may have been right. I said without hesitation, that if we were to be governed by the evidence presented, the man was. guilty. And the verdict was unanimous. The man was guilty. He was now suspended until the next annual conference, where his case was further looked into, and by the unanimous vote of the conference, he was expelled from, the church.

Now new responsibilities were imposed on me. The entire charge of the work was committed to my care. The circuit was large and I was without experience in the management of a charge and had never made out a report to read before conference. But my brethren were kind and I got through some way. I received a salary of $150.

CHAPTER III

In the fall of 1853 I was sent with G. C. Warvel—who had charge—to Mount Pleasant half station and Miamitown circuit combined. We preached every Sabbath at the former place and every two weeks on the circuit. We had some very interesting meetings this year. Bro. Warvel was a very stirring and quite a successful preacher.

There occurred an incident this year I must not fail to note: Grandfather Kumler for several years previously had made his home with my father, who resided two miles north of Mill-

ville—the place of my residence at that time.
I was in need of some money, (and this was the
condition of many of the itinerant preachers in
those days,) so I called on grandfather for
assistance. This was on Friday. He cheerfully granted the favor. I bade him farewell
and started for home. When about ten rods
from the house he came to the door and called
me to return. I at once did so, and when I entered the house he was sitting with his large
bible before him, and had already selected the
33d chapter of the book of Ezekiel. He read
at once about half of the chapter, where the
Prophet is speaking in impressive terms showing the responsibility of the watchman. He
then gave me a warm exhortation to be faithful
as a watchman upon the walls of Zion; to proclaim faithfully the counsel of God to the people. Then said he, "Now you can go; this is
all I wish of you."

I started to a protracted meeting on my
work, and on Monday following, while we were
enjoying a good meeting, a messenger came and
announced the sad intelligence of grandfather's
death. He had a severe stroke of the palsy

the next day after I had an interview with him, and fell asleep in Jesus on Sabbath, January 8, 1854, living only about one day after he was taken ill. A very short time, dear reader, you may say, for one to perpare for death, but not so in his case; he had been laboring for almost a half century in this blessed work of a chris-tian life, and death found him ready. My salary this year was $150.

Here is an incident in Bishop Zeller's life I should have given before: While on official tour he stopped at the town of M—— to have work done. The mechanic was a worthy man but would not attend church. While doing the work he looked at Bishop Zeller. He looked the second and the third time, but with strange feelings he could not account for. Another look, and conviction came into his soul. He had no rest (the stranger stood ever before him as he thought, praying for his poor soul,) till God spoke peace to him.

Another incident of the Bishop and his five brothers when they were boys: They lived a stream called Sweet Arrow. The family was poor, and often their meal consisted of a dish of soup. They would gather around this dish with spoons in hand and go for the soup, and as the contents of the dish would sink they would put down a spoon and measure it, and then say, "Sweet Arrow so deep," the dish of soup being compared to the stream.

After laboring two years in the Miami conference I moved into the bounds of the Sciota annual conference and settled in the village of Westerville, where our senior college is located. My object in doing this was to attend school and secure a better qualification for the work of the ministry. A Presbyterian minister by the name of Gilliland, with whom I had been long acquainted, advised me not to do this. Said he: "Persons who have deferred the work of drill and culture in college until they arrive at your age, and having the charge of a family, seldom succeed. I think you had better continue in the regular work in which you are engaged." I had made up my mind to go to school and to school I must go. And I need only say I entered college and applied myself to study as best I could for three years and a half, and while I might have succeeded better under other circumstances, I have never re-

gretted the course I took. After attending
school six months I was disappointed in my
financial arrangements and was out of college
for a time.

In the fall of 1855 I was ordained an elder
in Bethlehem church, Pickaway county, Ohio.
I was appointed by the Scioto annual conference
to a field of labor in Licking county, called the
Etna half station. Here I became acquainted
with Bro. J. M. Spangler, who was my Elder
this year. He was an open-hearted, cheerful
brother whom I dearly love. His kindness and
love toward me did much to introduce me to
the members of this conference. In leaving the
Miami conference I realized the sacrifice to be
much greater than I had expected. I had lived
twenty-eight in Butler county and had already
been a member of the church sixteen years and
was acquainted with a great many pious christians and enjoyed many happy seasons with
them. Now leaving all these and a large connection of relatives, including father and mother, four brothers and three sisters, and last
though not least the members of the Miami annual conference, bidding these all adieu and
going among strangers was no ordinary sacrifice.

But while all this is true I soon found that the same christian friendship and sympathy and religion prevailed among the membership and ministry of central Ohio. The first year's travel in Scioto annual conference although a pleasant year was not attended with such signal revival influence as the two former years in the conference I had left. This was a source of sadness to me and was the cause of close personal examination. This year's salary, $250.

But as I have already stated I spent three years and a half in school so at the close of this year's labor which was in the fall of 1856 I entered college again. I was now 30 years of age and there were five of us in the family and while there were difficulties with which to contend, mainly of a financial nature, I was enabled to continue three years in school and in the summer of 1859 completed the English course in the college. And while I am quite sure that my success was not what it might have been under other circumstances yet I shall ever prize highly these three years of mental drill in college. I doubt whether a young man can make a better investment, if he is a christian, than to secure a good education, and the more thorough

the better. These three years were pleasantly
spent. The noble hearted, intelligent christian
young men and ladies with whom I associated
and recited, will ever live in my most pleasant
memory of the past.

Among the most pleasant associations of
my life were enjoyed with the noble minded,
and kind hearted young men, and ladies of
Otterbein University. Among these we may
mention W. O. Hiskey, the Kumlers, the Hanbys,
the Haines, the Millers, Winters, and Clarks,
And then I must not forget, S. B. Allen, Henry
Garst, D. Surface, J. P. Landis and Guitner.
And the able faculty of the college—I have no
words that will express my appreciation of their
mental ability and moral worth. The venerable
and dignified President, Lewis Davis, who by
his own efforts of industry and habits of close
systematic study has distinguished himself as
an educator. Professor Walker, who had charge
of the Greek and Latin clasaes, was an eminent
teacher, and although quite impulsive in his
nature, excelled in his department of college
work. Professor Haywood, who occupied the
Mathematical chair, in view of his age and experience, was regarded second to none. He was

a very noble hearted man. There was but little
of the impulsive in his nature and all the students were much endeared to him. Professor
McFadden, who had charge of the department
of Natural Science, was a successful teacher
and quite much at home in his department of
labor. Afterward Professor Hammond was added to the faculty. Miss Gilbert, who was Prin-
cipal of the Ladies department, was a christian
lady and a successful teacher.

The college in the year 1854 when I entered
it was in its infancy, and the town of Westerville was a small place and its inhabitants were
favored with the music of the frogs, from morning until the morning again, the whole year,
with the exception of about three months during the winter season. The ponds which were
the homes of these interesting creatures, did
not add much to the health of the place. The
streets and sidewalks were in terrible condition,
and it had but few attractions for the visitor
who occasionally stopped there. But the work
of improvement soon commenced, and has been
gradually going on, and now after a period of
thirty-three years the town is one of the most
beautiful in central Ohio.

In June 1859 I completed the Scientific course in the college. This was an interesting occasion to me. The new college chapel was completed. It required extra exertions however to accomplish this. I remember I was induced to give fifty dollars in addition to what I had already given, so that it could be used for Commencement exercises. This was a large room 68x98 feet, and the ceiling about thirty feet high.

A large crowd gathered on Commencement day and this large room was filled to its utmost capacity. The trustees of the college and many visiting brethren from abroad were present to enjoy the exercises, and to see for themselves how well the graduates would acquit themselves. This added not a little to the interest of the occasion, and the friends of this school had anticipations of its success.

There were this year nine graduates: Two Scientific—Jacob Burgner and the writer; four who had completed the Ladies course—S. Leib, C. L. Slaughter, E. Walker and R. Bowman; and three who had completed the Classical course—S. B. Allen, J. A. Clark and John Holway.

In the month of September following, the Scioto annual conference held its session at Zion chapel, Perry county, Ohio. It was my privilege to attend it. We had a very pleasant session. Bishop Edwards preached a very stirring sermon from the text, "Open thy mouth wide and I will fill it." Truly God was with the preacher and in the midst of his people this holy Sabbath.

Brother E. Vandymark, one of the oldest ministers of this conference, was a very strong Liberty man; this could be said of the most of these ministers. He was so much interested in the anti slavery movement that when Fremont was candidate for President in 1856 he took a vow upon himself that he would not shave off his beard until Fremont was elected President of the United States. At this conference he had a long white beard which gave him a venerable appearance. I had let my beard grow for several years, not however that I had taken a vow upon myself so to do; but wore it for comfort and convenience. At this day there was a prejudice against christians wearing beards. One of the ministers of this conference who was an inveterate tobacco user, offered the following resolution for adoption by the conference: " Resolved, That the two brethren who wore beards be required to pass a razor over their faces so they might be distinguished from the Tunkers." Bishop Edwards, who up to this time had not worn a beard, arose to reply to this resolution. He remarked that he was not much in favor of ministers wearing beards, but after all is not the habit of using tobacco much more offensive in the sight of God than the beard?" He gave us one of his most elegant and stirring speeches against the use of tobacco. He alluded to the filthiness of the habit in defiling the house of God and in staining the mouth and bespattering the shirt bosom. These three so eminently applied to the brother who had offered the resolution that his countenance fell and he had not a word to say. The Bishop said he objected to the resolution because it was a very awkward one and also because it reflected on a christian denomination. I felt sure that the resolution would be lost, before the Bishop was half through speaking, and I was not mistaken, for it was lost without even one defending it, either by speech or vote.

At this conference I was assigned to the Pickaway circuit, with Joseph Hoffhines as my colleague. A number professed faith in Jesus and were received into the church. After I was appointed to this work a good brother by the name of Z. Morgan wrote me a kind letter and informed me that there would be objections to me for wearing a beard and that it would be better for me to take it off. He said a brother would leave the church unless I did. I thought at first it was unreasonable to sacrifice my beard to accommodate myself to the prejudices of one man. But afterward while meditating prayerfully over this matter, the language of Paul came to my mind, where he says: "If eating meat make my brother to offend I will not eat meat while the world stands." I shaved off my beard. I called on this brother who was so sensitive on this subject, and for a time things passed along with him pleasantly. It was not long however until there was something else that did not please him. One Sabbath as I was going into the church he requested me to present his name to the class for a letter of withdrawal from the church. I enquired of him the cause for this. He said there was too much

pride in the church and he wished to with-
draw. I presented his name to the class and
they gave him a letter. It was thought that
the real cause was kept back. The church
was needing a new roof and the brethren were
making arrangements to attend to this, and
it was thought he left the church to avoid the
responsibility that would devolve upon the
members of this society for this improvement.
So you see I lost my beard and my member
also. Those who have so little love for God's
cause will not accomplish much anywhere.'

This was my first year with a colleague in
which I had the responsibility of the charge of
the work. I had charge of a single work once
before.

This was only a little while after the John
Brown excitement at Harper's Ferry, Virginia.
My colleague called one stormy night at Kings
ton in Pickaway county, with an old United
Brethren family. He said to them that he was
a United Brethren preacher. "Well," said the
man, "I used to think a great deal of United
Brethren preachers, but since they are constantly striking and blowing for John Brown

I think but little of them." Soon after this the preacher was invited to another part of the house for supper, and his horse was put up for the night. It was late when he called, and by the time he had eaten his supper it was near nine o'clock. He then called the attention of the brother to the remark he had made about the preachers, and wished to know what he meant by it. "I mean," said he, "just what I said; these U. B. preachers are blowing for John Brown and I think but little of them." "Well," said the preacher, "who are striking and blowing for Brown?" "You are all doing it," was the reply. This chafed the preacher quite a little, especially when he repeated it, and said, "These mean abolition preachers are doing that very thing." The preacher inquired who it was. "You all do it," the brother said. "Well," said the preacher, "may be you think I am a mean man and blowing for Brown. He replied, "I have no doubt but you are." Said the preacher, "If you think I am a mean man I can not remain with you over night" "You can leave if you wish," was the reply. "Then," said our friend, "will you get my horse; I will be going." "Get him yourself

if you want him," was the retort. He gathered his wraps and started out to find his horse.
It was a very stormy, sleety winter night. The
good woman of the house sent a boy out to assist in getting the beast. And off he went, trav
eling through the storm about seven miles. It
was soon known all over town that he had
treated this preacher badly and it was not a
little to his discredit.

We had some precious revivals of religion
this year. It was a blessed time in my itinerate life. There were not less than fifty conversions and accessions to the church this year.
I traveled this year over three thousand miles
but I enjoyed good health, as also my family
was permitted to enjoy the same blessing. I received as salary this year not far from three
hundred dollars.

CHAPTER IV

In the fall of 1860 I was sent to the Etna and Burnside circuit with Samuel Longshore as my colleague. What used to be called the Albany circuit was connected with this work. This was the second time I traveled the Etna part of this work. Here I met the brethren and sisters with whom I had formerly worshipped and labored and I enjoyed myself among them very much. This year we had precious revivals of religion at Etna, Licking county, Ohio. These two meetings continued nine weeks; the former five and the latter four. They resulted in over seventy conversions and accessions to the church. We had some very good meetings at other points on this work; probably there were one hundred conversions and accessions to the church this year. Oh! these were blessed times never to be forgotten. Some of those who were converted this year have long since gone to the better land. Shall I meet them there?

The latter part of this conference year was a very exciting time. The great American Rebellion was being inaugurated. The flag at Sumpter had been fired upon by the rebels and the spirit of war was fanned to a flame. In May of this year General Conference convened at Westerville, Franklin county, Ohio. Secret societies, American slavery and the rebellion were the subjects of excitement and discussion by the conference. I received about $250.

In the fall of 1861 I was appointed to the Otterbein station. This is where I had lived over seven years and had spent half of this time in school. It was a responsible work and to take charge of a station where there was so much talent and learning was to me somewhat embarrassing; but by the sympathy and kindness of the ministers of the place, and the professors of the school I was enabled to continue during the year. I had much kindness and brotherly love shown me by Ex-Bishop Hanby.

He would say pleasantly to me: "Now, Brother
Zeller, when you get in a close place for some
one to preach for you then you can draw on
me." And so I did, for I seldom preached more
than once on the Sabbath.

Bro. J. Weaver who is now one of the
Bishops of the church, was soliciting agent of
the school and resided at this place. He was
kind, and ready to help me. President L. Davis
was also a good friend, and helped me much.
O! I shall never forget them. God grant that
their lives may be long and happy and their
deaths triumphant. And then here were the
learned professors of the college from whom I
had received instruction, and they were always
my bearers. I often felt that I should be the
hearer and that some one of the talented members of my congregation should be the speaker.
There were a few conversions and accessions to
the church during this year. Among the number was my oldest daughter, who was convert
ed and joined the church before she was twelve
years old. She was baptised by Brother Hanby.
Salary this year, $250.

In the fall of 1862 I was sent to the

Winchester circuit, which was mainly in the county of Fairfield Ohio. This was the stormy year of my itinerant life. There were a number of Pennsylvania Germans on this work, They were opposed to the war, and through the influence of their political leaders were made to believe that the preachers had brought about the war by their abolition doctrine, and some of them from the same cause would defend the system of American slavery itself.

I was invited by the brethren at Canal-Winchester to assist in holding a watch-night meeting. This meeting was held the night before the memorable first day of January, 1863, when the Proclamation of Emancipation issued by President Abraham Lincoln three months before, now liberated all the slaves in this great republic of ours. Now it would be expected that if there was any patriotism about us it would be stirred within us at such a time as this.

I met with the brethren agreeably with their request and being somewhat tired with my journey I rested until 8 o'clock. The class leader agreed to hold prayer meeting until that hour. We had a fine large brick church house in the village and this house was well filled, and the leader, L. C. was apparently enjoying himself well. I entered the house at the time appointed. I read God's word and the congregation sang with spirit and life. I felt at liberty in prayer, and asked God, in the lively exercise of faith to give us success in the meeting, and received hearty responses from the leader and others. But when I petitioned the Almighty to give the Union soldiers success in putting down the rebellion; and also asked tha all might enjoy the liberties we prized so dearly, I noticed the leader, responded no more, and indeed these last petitions offended the class leader, and as soon as prayer ended he left the house and said to a friend who met him on the street that he was going home and that he would not encourage these abolition preachers. This caused much excitement in town, and while the class was laboring to correct this brother for unchristian conduct, a charge of gross immorality was alleged against him. Two of the merchants of the town procured a warrant to have his house searched for stolen goods. They found the stolen property. He was then, arrested and tried and found guilty. He was afterwards expelled from the church. It was thought that the circumstances with which he was surrounded added not a little to his crime. He was in good circumstances. He had a good farm near town of two hundred acres worth sixty dollars an acre. This in addition to the loud profession of religion he had made for many years in the past added greatly to the crime.

At another point on the circuit the members proposed to give me a good salary if I would say nothing on the slavery question. I was unwilling to sell myself or my principles, either. I prepared a sermon on the subject of the christian's responsibility, and specified some of the things for which the christian would be held responsible. I dwelt upon the thought: We must oppose sin, and all sin of every kind; and if American slavery was a sin, there was but one course for the christian to take, and that was to oppose it. This offended the brethren much, and some one, I know not who, cut my harness, took off the burr from one of my buggy wheels and threw it away or hid it so I never found it, and well nigh disabled me from traveling. But after all this I continued upon the work, and filled my appointments and preached what I thought to be the truth as I should have to answer to God in the great jugdment day.

And now that the excitement is all over and passed I feel that I did the will of my Father in Heaven, and I trust the brethren alluded to have long since repented of their evil ways and see now that it was the will of God that slavery with its iniquity should come to an end. Brother S. Longshore was my colleague this year again, This good brother had been associated with the Democratic party. He was junior preacher on this work the previous year and the brethren at the class alluded to last, petitioned the conference to return him to this work. Their request was granted, and i was through him the bid was made to me to be silent on the slavery question. I spurned their offer and declared unto them the sin and iniquity of slavery. However they made good their threat to pay us but little salary. At the next quarterly meeting a wealthy class reported only one dollar.

Brother Joshua Montgomery, who was presiding elder, saw at once there was something wrong and inquired firmly what it was. Silence reigned for a time in the conference. The Elder pressed the question and after quite a delay the steward of the class remarked, "If I must tell, I must. The brethren of the Salem class (for this was its name) say they will not pay Abolition preachers." Brother Longshore up to this time had said nothing in the conference. Now he arose and remarked that his mouth had been gagged for about two years but now determined to take the gag off and be a free man. I give you now to understand that from the crown of my head to the soles of my feet I am an Abolitionist. Some of the members of the circuit said "We feared that Brother Sammy would be spoiled by associating with Zeller."

Such was the pressure brought to bear against this brother that he preached no more for this class. The quarterly conference passed a resolution asking them to pay us for the time we had labored for them, and if they desired it, we would labor for them no more. But they were unwilling to take the responsibility to say that we should stop preaching for them, so I continued to preach for them during the year and they supported me moderately well. Salary, about $200.

In the fall of 1863 I was sent by the con-ference to the Palestine circuit. Brother Dan-iel Bonebrake was my colleague. He was a most pleasant and agreeable companion. This year was much more pleasant than the last. We had gracious revivals of religion and there were over one hundred conversions and accessions to the church during this year. Brother Bone-brake had charge of the work. He held meet-ings at one end of the work and I did the same at the other end of the work.

I shall never forget a meeting I held near the town of Circleville, Pickaway county, Ohio. The meeting was continued about three weeks. James Blacker and wife were precious good christians. The former was class leader. They with only a few others labored faithfully with me. The meeting grew more and more inter-esting. I lodged part of the time with an ec-centric brother by the name of Capt. Ridge-way. One morning in the early part of the meeting, after arising from the slumbers of the night, he said to me: "Brother Zeller, we are going to have a good meeting." "Why," said I, "Captain, what makes you think so?" "O!" said he, "I had such an impressive dream last

night: I was near a stream that was almost
dry. And there were drift wood, brush and
trash along the bed of the stream. The water
commenced to rise and a large black snake
raised his head up through the drift, and he
made a wonderful hissing noise, and the water
in the stream raised higher and higher until it
swept away the snake, with all the drift, far in
the distance." Then he repeated again: "I
know we will have a good meeting." I told him
that I did not like to dream about snakes.

Whether this dream was an omen of a good
meeting or not I do not pretend to affirm. But
after all there was something in the progress of
this meeting like unto the dream: The stream
of salvation commenced to rise, and it rose
higher and higher and the drift of sin and iniquity was washed away. The work of the
Lord was graciously revived. Sinners were con-
victed and mourners were converted and christians rejoiced in the Lord. Indeed it was a
soul-cheering time for the Lord was with us,
and it is blessed to think of it yet.

An incident occurred at this meeting I
think will justify my relating: A wealthy fam-

ily lived near where the meeting was in session. They were very kind and clever. They invited me to make my home with them as much as I could or wished to, so I accepted their kind invitation and went with them frequently. They were members of the Episcopalian church in the city of Circleville. They were distant from their place of worship about five miles, and at this time were destitute of a pastor and seldom had services in their own church. So it was that they attended meeting with us quite regularly, took an active part in singing and were active members in the Sabbath school. In visiting with them I found that they were destitute of experimental religion of the heart and in conversing with them on this subject they would say as Nicodemus said to Christ: "How can these things be?" I tried to explain this subject to them and referred them to the teachings of the Bible on this subject.

But it is a difficult task to impress the mind of a formal professor of religion who has satisfied himself with the externals thereof, with the great importance of enjoying the life and power of God's grace in the heart. The lady of the house, who was very sociable and free to talk with me on this subject, one day gave me a hymn selected by her husband for me to read. This hymn told largely of the christian's doubts and fears and that this was an evidence that we were the children of God. I read the hymn carefully and then said to her: "This is only an opinion of a man. What is that in comparison to the teachings of the infinite God? He says, 'The spirit itself beareth witness with our spirits that we are the children of God.'—Rom. viii: 16. And again the apostle says, 'The love of God is shed abroad in our hearts by the Holy Ghost which is given unto us.'—Rom. v: 5. The Psalmist says, 'He brought me up also out of a horrible pit, out of the miry clay, and set my feet upon a rock, and established my goings. And He hath put a new song in my mouth, even praise unto our God.'—Psalms xl. 2. 'We know that we have passed from death unto life, because we love our brethren.'—1st John, iii: 14. These passages clearly teach us that it is our privilege to know that God is our friend in the forgiveness of our sins and that we are his children and heirs of Heaven."

There was a neighbor lady who was an intimate friend of the lady I am speaking about. and a member of the Methodist church. The name of the former was Mrs. Swearingen; and the name of the latter was Mrs. Rennick. As I was riding home with the S. family from meeting, after we were permitted to enjoy some excellent seasons of grace, we were conversing pleasantly together. Said Mrs. S.: "I do not like your prayer and speaking meetings. They are altogether different from our meetings. Your meetings for public preaching I enjoy wel enough; and my friend Mrs. R. says she is just like myself, and she is a member of the Meth. odist church." "Well," said I, "that's strange; the Methodists hold a great many of these kind of meetings." "Yes," said she, "I believe they do, but I could not take part in your speaking meetings; I could not get up in public and speak." I had requested her previously to take part in our social meetings. She appeared to take comfort from what her Methodist neighbor had said on this subject. She said the parents of Mrs. R. often insisted on her taking part in the social meetings but she could not. I said but little but thought a great deal about it: and this impression came forcibly to my mind: She can not be a live Methodist nor a live christian, either, or she would enjoy social religious meetings.

Up to this time there had been a few very clear conversions, but they were confined to the poorer class of people, and Mrs. S. would say, "If the work was among the higher class of people I would have some confidence in it." She inquired of a Presbyterian lady one night what she thought of the meeting and if she believed in experimental religion. Most assuredly I do, said the lady. This is the work of God's grace changing the heart.

About this time Mrs. S. and her husband were called away to attend the funeral of his father at Chillicothe. The meeting was growing more and more interesting daily, and before their return, their intimate friend, Mrs. R., became powerfully awakened and came forward trembling to the altar of prayer. I shall never forget with what earnestness and humility she asked the prayers of God's people in her behalf and with what meekness, simplicity and confidence she looked up to Jesus for salvation and although she was wealthy and well dressed she was humble and submissive as a child, and in a short time she was made completely happy. She obtained the pearl of great price and rejoiced in the love of Jesus. Now I needed no explanation why formerly she did not enjoy prayer and class meetings.

The next day we met for social worship again. In good time the sister was at the place of worship—and not as it was previously; now she sat near the stand among the lovers of Jesus. At rather a late hour Mrs. S. came to church also, having heard what had occurred the day before while she was absent, in the conversion of her intimate friend; but she took a seat far back in the house. I could not but be impressed with the contrast in the actions of these two persons who were much alike only a few days before. They invariably before sat together about the middle of the congregation. Now one was near the stand among christians, the other was far back in the house. I introduced the meeting by reading the 25th chapter of Matthew. Then after singing and prayer I commented awhile on the parable of the ten virgins. I then gave the privilege to all who

wished, to speak on the subject of religion.
Sister R. was the first to get up and speak.
She said: "I have been a member of the Methodist church for ten years and I never knew
what experimental religion was until yesterday.
I came forward to the altar of prayer and gave
my heart to Jesus, and O! how happy I am in
the love of the Savior. I will try to obey, love
and serve Him while I live."

We had a most precious season of grace
in waiting on the Lord that day. After a
number of the brethren and sisters had spoken
Mrs. S., who had refused to take part in speaking meeting and said privately she could not,
now arose in the back part of the house and
said: "I know these christian people enjoy
something to which I am a stranger. I fear I
will be like the foolish virgins of whom we
have been hearing to-day." She then with
tears in her eyes asked christians to pray for
her and then took a seat, manifestly with a sad
heart. She said to me afterward that she had
been a member of the Presbyterian church and
also a member of the Associate Reformed
church, and now to accommodate her husband
had joined the Episcopalian church, and she

thought she would not join any other. I said
to her that I would not insist on her to join any
other church, but I desired her to seek the salvation of her soul, that she might do good and
be happy and gain a home in Heaven when
done with this life.

The Swearingen family were very wealthy.
They had one thousand acres of land in the
Scioto valley, worth at the time of this meeting
one hundred dollars an acre. But with all this
it is to be feared they were destitute of the
riches of God's grace that makes the soul
happy.

At this meeting another wealthy man's
daughter was awakened and desired to seek religion, but was opposed by her parent. Her
father said to her if she went to the altar of
prayer and thus disgraced herself she could
not have a home with him. She was not permitted to attend the night meetings, but came
regularly to the day meetings. The spirit of
God so moved upon her heart that she came
forward to the altar of prayer and was happily
converted. So the Devil was cheated again by
christians having altar exercises and praying

and laboring with sinners in day time. I do not know all he did and said to his daughter by way of discouraging her; but the common report was that he did what he could to lead her in the way of sin and folly again. He secured some wicked worldly young people to induce her to attend a ball and thus to lead her away from Jesus and Heaven. O! what a fearful responsibility rests upon such parents; and what an awful account they must render by and by.

About three miles north of this place we had an extensive revival of religion. It was the continuation of the work of grace of which I have been writing. This meeting was commenced a few days after the close of the former one alluded to. Brother Bonebrake, my colleague, conducted the services mostly of this meeting and it resulted in many happy conversions to the christian religion. During the progress of this meeting, I commenced a meeting in the town of Palestine, which was a meeting of interest and power. There was much good accomplished at this meeting also, and many made happy in the Savior's love. A middle aged man of intemperate habits, sadly de-

graded, and deeply fallen, was made the subject of pardoning love; but I fear his old habits again obtained the ascendency and that the
went back to his cups again, and to filth and
degradation. O! what an amount of wretchedness and suffering the sin of intemperance has
brought upon the family of man.

Brother Bonebrake was with me during
the latter part of this meeting. After enjoying
a pleasant night's rest together, when we arose
in the morning, he remarked that he had a sin-
gular dream during the night: "I thought you
and I were fishing and you caught all the large
fish while I caught only small ones." We part-
ed from each other that morning and I thought
nothing more about the matter until Sabbath.
We had a very interesting meeting and I opened
the door of the church and received into her
five members of respectability who exerted
quite an influence in the community. When I
next met my colleague I said to him, I have
caught those large fish you had such an impressive dream about.

We had about one hundred and forty conversions and accessions to the church this year
and received three hundred dollars salary each,
and my travel this year was at least two
thousand miles, and my health was good and
God was my kindest and best friend.

CHAPTER V.

During this year the war of the American rebellion was raging fearfully and many noble young men were falling; some by disease and others on the battlefield. About the middle of May I was notified by the proper officer that I was drafted to go into the army. I had a large family, and my wife said it could not be that I should leave home, and go to war, and indeed such was the circumstances of my family at this time that it was very difficult for me to leave home. I made an effort to procure the money required for my release, but it was very

difficult to obtain it, A good hearted brother
by the name of D. Guitner who was engaged in
the merchantile business in the town of Westerville, agreed to let me have one hundred
dollars; and then I made considerable effort
to secure the remainder. There was an arrangement on the part of the goverment that by
the payment of three hundred dollars a drafted
man could be released. The times were quite
hard and money up to this time was scarce, and
I failed to get the remaining two hundred dollars. The time was at hand for me to report a
the headquarters of the military district, and
I was at a distance from the place eighty miles.
There were but two days left for me to get
ready to go at the call of my country, and one
of them the Sabbath day. The brethren requested me to preach for them as this would
be the last Sabbath I would in all probability
ever spend with them on earth. It was a solemn
time with me. I preached to a large congregation, Otterbein College, and the Lord was with
me. I bade them good bye.

On Monday morning I heard of a man who
lived six miles off, who had sold his farm, and

it was thought I could get money of him; but there again I was disappointed, and was returning home expecting to start to Mansfield, the headquarters of the militia, the next morning. On my way home a shower of rain came up and I stopped to shelter from the rain with a man who was somewhat acquainted with me. He had heard that I was drafted, and he inquired if it was correct. I told him that the report he had heard was true. "Are you going to war?" inquired he. I answered this is all that is left me. I am compelled to go. I can not secure the money and tomorrow I must report. He then said to me: You need not go, I will let you have the money. I need not say that I accepted his kind offer and with a light heart took the money and settled the account with the government, secured a receipt for the same and returned. My family was cheerful and much delighted that I was so kindly saved from a soldier's life, and it may be from a soldier's death. I have always regarded it as a special providence of God in directing me to where the money could be had.

I was now involved to a considerable extent financially and was paying ten per cent. in-

terest on my indebtedness. By close economy
I could sustain my family with the salary I received and what little I would make while at
home; but the interest I was paying yearly
was constantly increasing my indebtedness, and
with the very best I could do was getting more
and more in debt every year. I counseled with
my wife about this matter and suggested to
her that we had better sell the property we had
and purchase elsewhere. This was a great sacrifice for her to make. We had a good house
and the place and neighbors pleased her well.
We had now lived at Westerville and near the
place ten years. We had enjoyed the advantages of the college and good society all this
time. My children were of sufficient age to
enter high school and some of them had attended college some. Now we had to sacrifice
all these privileges if we left the place. We
decided however to sell out and try our fortune
elsewhere.

It was not long until I bought a farm
of one hundred acres for one hundred dollars
less than I sold my property for. This left me
still in debt about fourteen hundred dollars. I
did almost two men's work for a time, that is

as far as manual labor is concerned. I traveled circuit and did about as much as my neighbors farming; but this of course rendered me less useful as a circuit preacher, and I knew I could not long continue with such a heavy draft upon my physical structure. I had spent fifteen hundred dollars of my capital while I was in college three years. Four hundred of this, however, I donated to the school. Now I was anxious to get out or debt and I was trying hard by economy and hard labor to make this so I would have the same amount of capital I had ten years before, but this would have taken a long time had it not been for an advance in real estate. In just two years after I bought this farm I sold it for twelve hundred dollars more than I gave for it. This put me out of debt and I felt truly thankful for it. I moved upon this farm in March 1865. The winter previous was a very severe one. There was good sleighing awhile in February. Salary this year $250.

In the fall of 1864 I was returned to the Palestine circuit, with Oliver Spencer as my colleague. We had a pleasant time this year. The first day of 1865 was the cold New Years day. The weather for some time previous was mild and the day before it rained some. I commenced a meeting the night before at the Thomas chapel and announced a meeting for the next day. This was the most sudden and severe change in the weather I ever knew. At sundown it was warm, about ten degrees above freezing point. The next morning the mercury went down ten degrees below zero. A large amount of wheat was killed in central Ohio.

This cold day was on Friday and a few of us met for worship. The church house was somewhat open and it was impossible for us to keep comfortable. The part of a person next to a well heated stove was disagreeably hot and the other part was cold; so we suffered with heat and cold at the same time. It was thought on account of the very disagreeable weather we had better close the meeting.

I traveled seventeen miles the next day. Early on Saturday morning it was still bitter cold weather. I lodged New Years night with William Adams. I never came so near freezing while in bed in my life. I lay near a west window and although the house was tolerably good, the cold through the west window was so very piercing that all the sleep I had was in in the fore part of the night. I suffered so much with the cold that I got up and went d wn to the fire and spent the rest of the night by a good fire in conversation with the brother, I stopped with.

I had a horse and sulky with me but I started on my journey and walked ten miles before I rode any. I then rode about twenty-five minutes and became so cold that I was compelled to walk again. I did not ride at any one time that day more than one half hour. I arrived late at night, tired and hungry, at the house of George Goodson. He had the right name for he was a good, kind-hearted brother. He lived in Madison county, about eight miles from London, the county seat. This circuit was located in Pickaway, Franklin and Madison counties. I lived on the circuit and therefore my traveling was not so extensive. I received about $300 salary.

In the fall of 1865 the conference was held at Canal Winchester, Fairfield county, Ohio. I was sent this year to the Washington circuit, located near the county seat of Fayette county, and took its name from the county town of the same name. I only remained on this work one month; and this was the only field of labor I had ever left before my time expired. Brother Joseph Bybee, a very liberal hearted and wealthy man, supposed to be worth at least one hundred thousand dollars, lost all he had about the time I went to the work, by bailing his son. The year before, he paid about one third of the salary the preacher received. And his failing embarrassed the other brethren on the work. A brother of his who usually did well towards supporting the preacher, was seriously effected by his misfortune.

This was a small field and a few men supported their minister. Now this financial trouble coming upon them just at the time I went to the work, so completely discouraged them that they determined to do without a minister for a time. I ascertained this when I called a meeting of the officiary to arrange for the finance of the year. So when I heard their request and the reasons for the same, we pleasantly separated and I returned home.

Before I arrived at home when about five miles distant, I stopped where I was acquainted and applied for a school and conditionally arranged to teach. When I was within one mile and a half of home I was offered another position to teach school; and those of the former place being somewhat tardy in arranging the business of their school, I contracted to teach near home during the winter. I had preached the two previous years in the neighborhood where I contracted to teach.

A young man came to school who had formed the habit of profane swearing. The rules of my school forbade this ungentlemanly habit. And I made an arrangement with the directors that the young men and ladies who refused to obey the rules of the school should be dismissed by their authority. And the younger members of the school were to be entirely under my control. The young man alluded to had very bad training at home and I could not but anticipate trouble. I did what I could to learn his disposition and treat him accordingly. He was a high spirited young man and very impulsive in his nature but usually kind hearted and sociable. When he was angry his passions were uncontrolled, and then he was accustomed to use very bad language. I took pains to talk with him and tried to impress his mind with the ungentlemanly and also with the sinful course he was pursuing, and I tried to show him the very bad influence he was exerting among the children.

But all my efforts of moral suasion in his case failed. And by the authority of the directors I informed him that he must leave school. He took his books and left us, and I supposed my trouble with him was now at an end. But in this I was sadly mistaken. His father interceded with the directors, and obtained premission for him to return again; with the understanding however that he should be under my control, and that in case he should violate the rules of the school I should inflic corporal punishment upon him. I feared the consequences for his father was a neighbor of mine, and a very profane man himself.

It was not long after this until he became angry again, and used bad language. He had intimated some days before to the boys that I was not man enough to inflict punishment upon him. In this however I had no difficulty; for I chastised him severely. He left the school

and did not return. I felt sad at the thought
that the friendship of this family, and especially of this young man, was now at an end,
probably forever. But I was agreeably mistaken in this. At a quarterly meeting held
subsequently he came forward penitently to
the altar of prayer, and ever afterward treated
me with kindness and respect. I believe it did
him good.

During the spring and summer I worked
on the farm part of the time and part of the
time - sold books. During this summer my
oldest daughter, M. E. Zeller, taught her first
school.

In the fall of 1866 the conference was held
in Vinton county, Ohio, not far from McCarthy
town, the county seat. From this conference
I was sent to the Walnut circuit. At this conference I made my first effort to preach before
the Bishop and the other members of the conference. The walnut circuit was situated in the
counties of Fairfield and Pickaway. It was a
large work. I had eleven appointments and
considerable traveling to do this year. There
were some conversions and accessions to the

church. A very intelligent and influential young man by the name of Whitehead was awakened and embraced religion this year. Sometime after the meeting closed we attended to the ordinance of baptism. At the close of services in the church I gave an opportunity for those who recently embraced religion to come forward and take a seat near the stand and I would ascertain their names and the way they wished to be baptized. A number came forward. Some wished to have the ordinance attended to by sprinkling, one by immersion. The young man alluded to, when I enquired of him how he wished to be baptized, replied that he wished to go to the water. We went to a nice clear stream near by. Several knelt down by the stream and I baptized them by sprinkling water upon them. I then enquired of this young man again how he wished to be baptized. He replied that he would go into the water and kneel down and I should pour the water on him. I did so and we had a very pleasant time.

Now, dear reader, we went to the water and from it; and we also went into the water and came up out of it, and attended to the ordinance of christian baptism, as far as we have any evidence, in a scriptural way, and there was no immersion as far as these were concerned. After these were baptized we went still a little farther into the water and baptized by immersion. And after all there was but one Lord, one faith, one baptism.

When I first went to this work I formed an acquaintance with a local preacher by the name of Philip Lamb. He was a good hearted brother but somewhat peculiar. I think he was the most uneven in his christian life of any man I ever knew. At times he would be on the mountain top of extacy and enjoyment and then in the valley of gloom and despondency. His oldest daughter, Sarah, by name, was the opposite of her father; even tempered and apparently always happy. She was afflicted with consumption. She was much resigned to the will of her Father in Heaven. In conversation with her she often said: "It is all right if I live; or, if I die it is all right." She grew worse and while I was holding a meeting near by she died a most triumphant death. The night before her death a number of her young classmates remained with her all night. She became very anxious to hear singing early in the morning. She said to her friends that she would like very much to hear them sing: and to hear them sing the hymn:

> "I am glad that I am born to die,
> From grief and woe my soul shall fly."

They sang the hymn all through, and she requested them to continue singing. They then started to sing some other hymn. She asked them to stop, and said to them · "I want you to sing, but I want you to sing the same good hymn you sang before." And they repeated it over and over until she left the world in triumphs of faith and a glorious hope of endless life in Heaven.

In April of this year I moved to Fairfield county, on the work I was traveling, about five miles from the city of Lancaster. This is an old settled country. Among the first improvements made in this state were here and at Marietta. Here I resided two years and six months; and sold for an advance of seven hundred dollars above what I paid. I received this year $350 salary. I and my family were much blessed with health.

CHAPTER VI

In the fall of 1867 the conference was held at the Howser church, near Etna, close to the line between Licking and Fairfield counties. Here I was appointed to the Logan circuit. This was in the vicinity of the county seat of Hocking county and derived its name from the town. I never had such severe temptations during my itinerate life as in the first two weeks after my appointment to this work. Some unguarded expressions from one of the members of the conference, and my removal from the Walnut circuit, was the main cause of this terrible gloom and sadness. I had moved only a few months before forty-five miles on the work I was traveling; and now to be sent thirty miles farther on appeared to me to be very hard, but this was not the lightest part of my temptation. I thought one of my best friends had turned against me. Like David, I felt, if an enemy had done this I could have borne it; but a friend to lift up his heel against me, was too much. I worried over this matter until it became worse and worse. I then resolved to write the brother a letter. He came at once to see me and made it all right. He acknowledged his fault in doing me a wrong and he left me with his best wishes and I have ever since felt that he was a good man and have now the kindest feelings toward him.

I went to the Logan circuit and it was one of the best years of my life. I commenced a meeting two miles north of Logan, at the Bethany church. The Lord was with us to awaken sinners and comfort mourners. And christians were greatly revived at this meeting. There was a number of additions to the church by profession of faith in Jesus Christ. The next meeting was commenced northwest of Logan four miles, at Pleasant Hill church. A local preacher said to me, "I do not think you will succeed at this place, it is a hard place to do anything. B. Hood made an effort and failed, and he was a good revival preacher." "Well," said I, we will hold a meeting and leave the event with the Lord." I prevailed on the brethren to hold a meeting a few days before I could be there, and the second time I preached for them the way was opened for the anxious souls to come to the altar of prayer. Several came forward at once and we had a precious meeting and many were converted to living faith in Jesus.

A young lady by the name of Isabel Iles, who was living with her uncle Wm. Iles, became awakened and was very anxious to have her uncle take her to the meeting. After she had asked him several times he concluded to take her to the meeting. He was not a christian himself. The first time she attended the meeting as soon as the invitation was given, came forward to the altar of prayer and was made the subject of saving grace. I shall never forget with what speed she went back in the congregation and threw her arms around her uncle's neck and told him of the joys of salvation and besought him to give his heart to Jesus and be happy also. I think through her pious life he was led to the Savior; for it was not long until he too was the subject of saving grace. Oh! this was a blessed time of comunion with God and with his people.

Some years after, I received a telegram from the family to be present with them and preach the funeral sermon of this christian lady. I got on the Hocking Valley railroad and went to where the family lived. There was a large number of neighbors and friends at the house and they expected their pastor present also. To meet their wishes, I preached at the house where they lived. Some of the family were sick and could not go to the church. We then went in procession four miles to the grave yard and church house: and here was a large congregation, and they requested me to preach again to the people. This was the first time in my life that I preached two funeral sermons, and partly to the same congregation for the same person on the same day.

During the revival meeting just alluded

so I visited a family by the name of Tignor. We were sitting cheerfully around the fire engaged in social conversation when I was impressed to speak to a young man of the family about the interests of his soul. I said to him, "David, do you not think that you ought to be a christian?" He answered very promptly, "No sir, I think not." I replied to him, "Well, David, I am sorry to hear this." The next night he came to the altar of prayer and anxiously, sought the pardon of his sins and was made happy in the Savior. I said to him after his conversion that he was like the son in the gospel, who said to his father, who told him to go into his field and work: he said he would not go, but afterwards repented and went. This was preferable to the course taken by the other son who said, I go sir, but went not.

On Saturday of the first week of the meeting I called on Brother J. Iles to conduct the meeting over the Sabbath or to fill my appointments on the lower part of the work. He decided to carry on the meeting. On Saturday night he preached for the people and was considerably embarassed, and the members complained some that I had left, and this

tempted the good brother to think they did not
want him to preach for them. He told them he
would not be with them the next day; but he
had already announced his appointments for
Sabbath. He made his statement good to them,
for he remained at home and did not not attend
the meetings for nearly a week. I told him I
would not return until Monday. While I was
on my way to my afternoon appointment I resolved to make an extra exertion to be at the
meeting again Sabbath night before they would
close. I had twelve miles to ride after four
o'clock. At about seven o'clock I drove up to
the meeting house. I at once saw there was a
large congregation out. But it was so strange
to me that everything was so very quiet in the
house. There was no singing and everything
was as still as death. I expected that Bro. Iles
would be preaching, or if he had closed this
part of worship, they would be laboring with
the anxious, and I could not think what was
wrong. I hitched my horse as soon as I could
and went in. The class leader and exhorter
were counseling what to do with the meeting.

I went into the pulpit and took for my
text the 6th verse of the 55th chapter of Isa-

iah: Seek the Lord while He may be found; call upon Him while He is near. I talked from these words about thirty minutes, enforcing the conditions of the text as well as I could, and then presented the altar of prayer, and invited penitents to come forward and engage with us in prayer and there were several who availed themselves of this privilege, and some who had not been at the altar, before, and we had a blessed time all that week. On Tuesday I think I never enjoyed a better meeting. There were four young men who had been anxiously seeking religion for several days. They all professed faith in Jesus, and then we had a rejoicing time together indeed.

These meetings continued over five weeks and from the first invitation given to penitents to come forward to the altar of prayer until the last at the close of the meetings, there were penitents who availed themselves of this privilege at each invitation thus given. This made an impression on my mind as being something more than common.

I then commenced a meeting about eight miles south of Logan, at the New Zion church,

and in one week from its commencement there
were twenty-two who professed faith in Jesus
in the forgiveness of their sins. And here again
as it was at the other two meetings, every time
an invitation was given to penitents they came
to the altar of prayer. This meeting progressed
with the least effort of any I ever held; but I
fear the work of grace was not as permanent as
many others. Some however who embraced
religion at this meeting proved faithful and I
have reason to believe did an honor to the
cause of the Master and at last found a home
in the better land.

I commenced a meeting in the latter part
of March at the Fellowship church, about five
miles east of Logan. I drove into the neighborhood a little before sunset on the Sabbath day.
I told a few who were near that we would have
meeting there that night. It was called afterwards a surprise meeting, for no one was expecting it. Here again the Lord was with us
in awakening and converting power. Some ten
or twelve professed faith in Jesus. A man of
family by the name of Gilbert Donaldson, who
had been seeking peace with God through Jesus for five years, was happily converted at this

meeting. He obtained peace in believing at a speaking meeting on Sabbath morning. We had a very precious meeting that day. Truly the Lord was with His people on His holy day.

A few minutes before the time for preaching had arrived, Bro. Donaldson arose in the congregation to express himself on the subject of religion and while speaking, the Lord powerfully blessed him; and then his talk was so much more impressive on the minds of the people than anything I could have said that I resolved not to interrupt him. He did the most impressive pleading with sinners to give their hearts to Jesus and to be saved by His grace I ever heard. Now as his preaching was so much in advance of what I could have done I recalled my appointment for preaching and told the brethren and sisters that they should do the preaching at that hour; and they did it right well, for God was with them to help them. There was another middle aged man who had long been seeking the pearl of great price and who found it to the joy and comfort of his soul, and went on his way rejoicing.

I was more than ever impressed with one feature of these meetings already alluded to, namely : that every time I had invited sinners to come to the altar of prayer, from the first of December until April, there was one or more who without delay came forward and anxiously sought for the forgiveness of sins. There were penitents seeking religion at each of these meetings when they closed. This is an occurrence which it has never been my privilege to see and enjoy before nor since this time. Truly the Lord was very near and very precious to me all this time.

There were about sixty conversions and not quite so many accessions to the church this year. I traveled not less than sixteen hundred miles. The providence of God toward me made a deep impression on my mind. I went to this work under severe temptations and with a heavy heart. I felt that in the removal from the work I had traveled the year before great injustice had been done me, and while it was the darkest year of my life at the beginning, it was in the outcome the brightest and the best. And thus it is, God leads us in a way that looks dark and strange to us, but after all it is the way of kindness and mercy to us. Salary about $250.

In the fall of 1868 the conference was held at Westerville, Franklin county, Ohio. At this conference I was sent to the Pleasant Run circuit. This was convenient to where I lived. This circuit was located in Fairfield county, near Lancaster. There were five appointments on this work and either of them could be reached in two hours drive. In December of this year I moved into the city of Lancaster. This town is one of the oldest in the state. I believe Marietta was settled awhile before. Mount Pleasant is situated near the city on the north side. This is a hill two or three hundred feet high. Its sides on the south, west and north are almost perpendicular. On the east it is gradually sloping so that it may be easily ascended from this side. From the top of this mount a splendid view may be had of the city. This hill is noted as the place where Wetzel had a hard struggle with the Indians. Here he rescued a young lady who had been a captive with the Indians a long time. It was on this hill where he defended himself and the young lady. It is said he rolled a large stone from this hill which frightened them, and escaped unharmed with his prize. The fair ground is located on the west immediately at the foot of the mount. Hundreds of visitors ascend this hill at fair times. My family attended religious meetings at the M. E. church. We were about two miles distant from the nearest appointment on this circuit.

We had a very pleasant time associating with christians in this city. Church and Sabbath school were very convenient. I preached in the M. E. church quite frequently during this year; once for the colored people, by invitation. We had a pleasant time, indeed their singing excelled anything I had heard for some time. I shall not soon forget Bro. B. N. Sparr who was pastor of the congregation part of the time; and Bro. Taylor who was pastor the rest of the time we lived in the city.

Bro. Jonathan Rarick who made no profession of religion was superintendent of Sabbath school at the Pleasant Run class. When the minister the previous year made an effort to organize a school there were none found in the class who were willing to superintend the school. Mr. Rarick proposed to take charge of the school. This was opposed by some of the older members, on the ground that he was not a professor of religion. He was elected

however by a large majority of the class. He
commenced in good earnest and soon had one
of the best schools they ever had before in
that class. When I went to the circuit there
was objection urged by some of the old members against Mr. Rarick conducting the school.
They said it was a disgrace to the church that
one who makes no profession of religion should
lead the school. I told them they had none to
blame but themselves. I advised them to as
sist in making the school as interesting as it
could be made. They all became interested
and worked faithfully and we had a very
pleasant and profitable time. The superintendent was atheoretical christian, and would say to
me when I would converse with him on this
subject that he desired to be an experimental
christan and to enjoy the blessings of sal-
tion.

We commenced a protracted meeting at this
place. The meeting grew in interest and a
blessed work of grace commenced in the hearts
of the people the second week. Some of the
Sabbath school scholars were the first to give

their hearts to the Savior. I visited Bro. Rar-
rick at his home and urged upon him the
claims of religion and told him it would be a
good help to him in instructing the children
if he were to enjoy the blessings of salvation
himself.

While I pressed this motive upon his attention he said to me he knew he ought to be a
christian. He then inquired of me if I did not
think that he could, by using the means of
grace, singing and praying with christians, obtain the blessing of pardon and peace. I replied if he had humility and contrition of soul
sufficient to make any sacrifice Jesus required
of him he might obtain the blessings of salvation; for this blessing was designed for all
who would meekly and humbly go to Jesus
and call upon him in the exercise of living
faith; for it was through the atoning merits of
Jesus alone that men could have the forgiveness
of their sins and the regenerating power of
God's grace in their souls. Now if he was unwilling to humble himself as much as it requires
him to do in going to the altar of prayer, he
would likely fail to obtain the blessing he desired. The humility and reproach of the cross

of Christ was the real difficulty in his way and it required quite an effort on my part to make him see it, and I should have utterly failed had it not been for the divine light of the grace of God shining upon his mind.

An interesting boy and the only child of his, sixteen years of age, was awakened and at the altar of prayer was made the subject of God's pardoning love. In his conversion we had a clear evidence of the power of saving grace, and this added much to the interest of the meeting. A few nights after this while we were laboring with penitents at the altar of prayer I called on him to lead in prayer, as he had suggested this as a probable war of success. I concluded to try it, but this was an entire failure, his mouth was closed, he could not utter a sentence. This was used as a means by the Holy Spirit to humble him before the Lord.

I preached the next night from the circumstance of Naaman's unwillingness to comply with the conditions the prophet gave him to effect a cure. As soon as I gave an opportunity for penitents to come forward to the altar of

prayer, he at once, came to the altar and plead
for mercy, and the same night after service in
the church, he went home and while anxiously
looking to Jesus in the exercise of faith obtained the forgiviness of his sins. This meeting
continued four weeks and there were about
twenty who professed faith in Jesus and were
added to the church.

In February of the same year he took the
contract to build the bridge across Eel river
near Bowling Green, Clay Co., Ind. At this time
the United Brethren had a weak society near
the river where he had his contract. The brethren had an old log church house, and it was
with them indeed the day of small things. Bro.
J. Barrick organized a sabbath school and in a
a little while he had the best school in all that
country. The Lord blessed their efforts and
they had from time to time good revivals of religion, and about two years after, the brethren
built a new house, and they now have a flourishing society, and much of their prosperity is owing to the efforts of J. Barrick in the sabbath
school. After my removal to Illinois I traveled
this work and he was then talked of as the best

sabbath school worker that had ever been in that country. The objection to his conducting sabbath school was now all removed, and he was elected class leader and served in this capacity with acceptability. O! how interesting, it was to see the superintendent and the scholars of the school side by side together seeking religion, and what was better still, to know that they had consecrated themselves to the service of the Lord and was happy in His love.

I had a very interesting meeting this year at the appointment near Baltimore, Fairfield county. The meeting was a little dull in the commencement, but the Lord came to our help and through Him we triumphed gloriously. Sinners were awakened and some professed faith in Jesus. One evening while we were laboring with penitents at the altar of prayer a young man by the name of Henry Devenbaugh fell as suddenly as if he had been shot through the heart. Some said he was dead. I went to him and he was cold and stiff. I believe he could have been taken up by the head and feet without his body bending a particle. We took him to the nearest home and he remained much the same way—just like a dead man—only he was much more stiff and cold than any dead man until morning. This condition of things then passed away and he became material again There were two others effected in the same way during this meeting. I received this year $485 salary.

The quarterly conference at its last session unanimously asked for my return to this circuit by passing a resolution to this effect, but this was the last I traveled circuit in Ohio.

CHAPTER VII

In the fall of 1869 the conference was held in Circleville, Pickaway county, Ohio. At this conference I was elected Presiding Elder and placed upon the Rushville district. This district had fields of labor located in nine counties, as follows: Fairfield, Perry, Muskingum, Morgan, Washington, Meigs, Athens, Vinton, Hocking. I had eleven fields of labor, nine circuits and two missions. Their names were as follows: Bloomington, Portland, Willowcreek, Cedarville Mission, Marshfield Mission, Gibersonville, Pleasant Run, Rushcreek, Deavertown, Plymouth, Logan.

During this conference I had a home assigned me with a brother of very limited circumstances. I was well satisfied with my home. The members of the family were kind but they were very poor. After I was elected P. E. the station preacher, the previous year, came to me and said he wished me to go and be the guest of a wealthy banker during the rest of the conference. Said he, It will not do, you know, for the reputation of our conference to send any of our ministers to such a place; I think you should be the banker's guest. He has requested that some of the ministers stop with him. Yes, said I, When we were appointed our homes, any place would do for Zeller, but now as I have been promoted by the conference you come around with your compliments and blarney. I think I had better not change my boarding place. It will make those feel bad with whom I am stopping. Said he, I am well acquainted with them and will see them and make it all right.

After being earnestly pressed to make the change, and being assured that the station preacher would make it all right with the family with whom I was stopping, I consented. I was then the guest of the wealthiest man in the city of Circleville. Some of his family were members of the Episcopalian church; but as for himself I fear he trusted in his wealth. He would converse upon the subject of religion in a general way, and spoke of Rev. William Otterbein, founder of our church, in the highest terms; and with whom he said he was well acquainted while he lived in the city of Baltimore. I suppose after all it was best that the change was made, at least this poor family had a little more bread and meat left for their own wants than if I had remained: while the rich banker had an abundance left, if he was not in any other way benefitted by the change. Giving that little might soften his heart some.

Circleville is one of the most beautiful towns in central Ohio, with a population of about 5,000. The country around the city is the most beautiful and productive, and taking everything into account, it is the best country I ever saw. The Scioto valley and the Pickaway plains can not be surpassed any where.

In the fall of 1870 we met in annual conference on the Gibersonville circuit, about five miles north of Logan, the county seat of Hocking county, Ohio. Bro. J. J. Glossbrenner presided. We had a very interesting session of conference. Bro. J. W. Sleeper, a very cheerful and sociable fellow, was one of the presiding elders, and William McDaniel the other. Bro. J. W. S. came to me and remarked that he had the best report of any of the presiding elders this year. I replied to him: We will figure up and see. The result of casting up the figures is as follows:

Bro. William McDaniel, Winchester district.—Accessions to church, 447; missionary money collected, $591; salary, $690.

J. W. Sleeper, Cynthiana district.—Accessions to the church, 1032; missionary money collected, $395; salary, $651.

S. W. Zeller, Rushville district.—Accessions to the church, 1105; missionary money collected, $7.0; salary, $640.

This being my first year as presiding elder, I thought but little of the result of my labor until this good brother introduced the matter. This result was not so much owing to my labor as it was to the faithful ministers of my district.

During this year my family was seriously afflicted. The two youngest of the family came very near dying. While the older of the two was very low with typhoid pneumonia I was more than a hundred miles away from home. After the physician did what he could, he became somewhat excited and wished to know where I was, and said to my companion he had doubts of her recovery, and that I ought to be informed of her condition. Active efforts were made use of to get word to me, but I failed to receive the sad news until she had partially recovered. And then the youngest was also quite sick, but the good Lord kindly spared their lives and raised them to their usual health again.

At this conference I was elected presiding elder and sent to the Cynthiana district. In this district there were fields of labor located in eleven counties, as follows: Fayette, Ross, Pike, Highland, Adams, Scioto, Lawrence, Galia, Jackson, Vinton and Hocking. I had twelve fields of labor,—eight circuits, two stations and two missions, as follows: Cynthiana station, Ironton Mission station, Bear Creek, Hillsboro,

West Union, Scioto, Burlington, Centerville, McArthur and Hallsville, and Wilkesville and Raysville missions.

This year was very pleasant in the main. We had extensive revivals and many precious souls added to the church of Jesus Christ. Living, however, at Lancaster, the county seat of Fairfield county, in the bounds of the work where I had traveled the year before, I had necessarily a large territory to travel over, and was from home from three to six weeks at a time.

How wonderful are the providences of God! Things that have been very trying to our natures: and during the lapse of years have almost been forgotten by us, come up again with different phases, sometimes favorable and at other times only to deepen the wound and add to our sorrow. I had learned from the good book that he who hateth suretyship is sure: and realizing the effects of not heeding the wise man's counsel, in that I bailed three student gentlemen who were in close quarters financially, while I was attending Otterbein University, and having part of the money to pay. This occurred about the year 1857. As I was engaged in my regular work, I went to hold quarterly meeting in the place where the father of one of the student boys lived. While in conversation with the family I incidentally learned this fact. I was considerably surprised at this, for I never expected to see the student again, much less his father and mother. Of course I was anxious to know what had become of their son. They informed me that he went into the army six or seven years before and that he had lost his life in defence of his country.

I merely alluded to this business transaction, and his father voluntarily without asking him for it, paid the claim. When he proposed to do this, I said I could not say his son was the one who really owed the debt. I had bailed the three and had the money to pay. He replied that he had heard his son say just before he went into the service of his country that there was a claim of this nature unsettled, and that he was anxious to have it settled. This did a good deal to change my mind with reference to these three student boys. I had now learned for the first that this young man had assumed the debt, and it may be, arranged for his father to pay the debt. I did not inquire after this, but the cheerful manner in which he paid it impressed me this way.

During this year I bought a horse of a brother in whom I had the utmost confidence, that caused me quite an amount of trouble and not a little suffering. The beast was recommended to me as being all right. I hitched him up in my gig, in which I traveled this year, and drove him about five miles without any trouble, when the animal commenced all of a sudden to kick, without any apparent cause, and broke my rig considerably; but the worst of all inflicted a wound on me that was painful and annoying for weeks, and came near being a very serious affair with me. Here I was five miles away from the place where I got the horse, and for a time I did not know what to do. In my extremity a man came along and said he knew the horse well, and that he would often take such spells and without any apparent cause would kick everything to pieces, and that doubtless the man I had got the animal of knew it. I decided at once to send the horse back to the man I got him of.

The greatest trial I had to endure this year was with reference to troubles arising from charges preferred against one of the traveling preachers on my district. When I came to his field of labor I ascertained that there was a good deal of excitement about the matter in the community. When we entered into the business of the quarterly conference the preach- er introduced the matter himself and said he would investigate the matter, and because I in- sisted on the conference to take the disciplin- ary steps in the investigation of his case, but more especially because I intimated to some of the brethren that there had been trouble with him on the same line before; he became my in- veterate enemy. He succeeded in getting a committee that was one sided, and in his favor, who decided that there was no cause for action in his case. The charge was a grave one and there was sworn testimony against him, and yet the committee decided that there was no cause for action against him. I have reason to fear that deep, dark iniquity was covered up in this case. This must be left however for the judgment day to reveal. O what an amount of deep-laid schemes of iniquity and deception will be exposed in the great day. It is believed that the same man obtained holy orders for the ministry by telling a disgraceful lie on his first wife, from whom he was separated, and marrying another previous to entering the ministry

Some time before this I had arranged to go west and this forbade me taking any active measures in his case. I am quite sure if I had remained in the conference I could not have permitted this matter to have passed by without at least an investigation. I have no ill feelings toward this brother but hope that if he is guilty he will see the importance of making this matter all right before his probation ends. And if I have been uncharitable in anywise towards him I desire forgiveness; but after 12 years have elapsed since these things have occurred I see no reason to change my mind on this subject. My salary this year was $600, and I think in other respects the reports compared favorably with the year before. Soon after this I closed up my work in Scioto annual conference, being connected with it from September 1854 to the latter part of August 1871; almost seventeen years.

In the fall of 1871 I joined the Lower Wabash annual conference. Its session this year was held in the city of Terre Haute, Ind. I had not been in the city for over twenty years. In the year of 1846 I visited this town. It was then a small place. In walking down through the city from 14th street to the river on the same thoroughfare I had traveled 26 years before, I could scarcely believe my own eyes when I looked at the wonderful change that was brought about by the energy and skill of man. Terre Haute had grown from a village probably of 1,500 to a city of 25,000 in the short time of 26 years.

Rev. David Edwards was the presiding Bishop, and with some little exception we had a pleasant time. On Sabbath in the morning services were held in the M. E. Centenary church. This is a very fine building. By invitation I introduced the morning services. We had an interesting hour in the relation of christian experience and in singing spiritual hymns to the praise of God. The Bishop then preached a very stirring sermon from the cir—

cumstance of the children of Israel being fed for over forty years, miraculously with manna from heaven.

I was sent this year to the Center Point circuit, located in Clay county, Ind. I went to my work determined to do the best I could for the welfare of immortal souls and for the honor of God's cause. I had a discouraging time; for it was sixty miles to the first appointment. I found kind brethren on the work, and we had good meetings and some ingathering into the church. In the fall of the year I met with a number of the members of the conference in a ministerial association for the first time. This meeting was held at Rosehill, Vigo county, Ind. Here we had lively discussions on female suffrage and other interesting topics. Our worthy Bishop did not endorse woman suffrage. He feared the better class of women would remain at home while the baser sort would avail themselves of this privilege, if it was granted them to vote.

The winter following was exceedingly cold and I was absent from home nearly all the time. My oldest boy who was in his fourteenth year, exposed himself quite too much, not being accustomed to the severity of the western winds. I fear his fatal afflictions were induced from a want of care after exercising, which caused serious lung trouble. He was taken down on the 12th of February, with the fever. When I left home he was well as usual, and I thought enjoying good health. But the attack was very sudden and severe. I am under the impression that a mistake was made in his treatment. The doctor advised the application of cloths wet with cold water on his breast; and I think this was not carefully attended to, and it threw him into a congestive chill, which came very near proving fatal at once, and from which he never recovered.

I was at once sent for, and when the messenger came, although he was not from the neighborhood where I lived, I was forcibly impressed that there was something wrong at home. I was informed that my boy was seriously ill. I started at once and although it was very difficult to travel on account of the ice, I arrived home the same night, which was Thursday. He suffered intensely the rest of the time he lived, and died a little after midnight on Saturday morning.

But it was a very cheering thought that he had embraced religion over a year before. The evening before I left home, which was just one week before I returned, I called on him to lead in family devotion and he prayed with more freedom than I had ever heard him. I was so glad to believe that in his youthful days he was trying to love and serve the Savior. Arrangements were made for the interment of his body, and it was laid away to await the resurrection morning. This was a sad affliction for us. He had arrived at an age to be a great deal of cheer and comfort to us. O how often I thought of him and the happy hours we spent together. But we could only say the Lord giveth, and taketh away, blessed be the name of the Lord.

We had five children remaining—four girls and one boy: of the former three were the oldest of the family; and I felt thankful that it was no worse with us. During this year we had four children in college and paid eighty dollars for their tuition, besides incidental charges, and expenses for their books, and clothing for the family. I received as salary $220, and spent about six hundred. Thus ended the first year of itinerant labor, in the Lower Wabash annual conference.

In the fall of 1872 the Wabash annual conference held its session at New Goshen, Vigo county, Ind. I received for my appointment this year the Westfield circuit. This year I had some of the severest trials of my life. It had been only one year since I moved to Westfield, Ill., and the greater part of this time I spent sixty miles away in Indiana; and of course was but little known. One thing favorable, my work was near where I lived. I went out on my work with a good deal of cheer. This was the year of the great epizootic among horses. Farmers were fearful that travelers would be the cause of spreading this disease, and that their horses would take sick and die. So part of the year I traveled afoot, and indeed part of the time my horse was affected with the same trouble. And when I took my horse at times it had to be left at a distance from other horses. But farmers soon ascertained that it made but little difference whether their horses were exposed to the disease or not; for alike nearly all the horses in the country took it. But only a few of them died, and the excitement died away.

At the close of this year the village of Westfield had the severest scourge of typhoid fever that was ever known in this region of country. On the 13th of August our second daughter was taken down with it. And then we had constant watching and waiting on the sick members of our family, until about the 25th of October; during which time we buried our three oldest children. And for some time we thought we would have to bury the fourth one; but a kind providence smiled upon us, and she was spared for our cheer and comfort. This left us two children, one twelve, and the other nine years of age. This was a very sad time with us. To be called upon to part with our three oldest children, all of whom were grown, and aged respectively, twenty-three, twenty-one and nineteen, was a trial exceedingly severe; but the good Lord was with us, and gave us strength and grace to endure it. My salary this year was $100, and our expenses were not less than $800.

This siege of affliction continued some time into the next conference year. The conference in the fall of 1873 was held in Westfield where we were living. And during its session two of the girls were lying in a very critical condition, and on Wednesday after its close the oldest one died. And in a little over three days after this the second died also. At this time the third one showed some signs of taking the fever. We secured a physician who we called as counsel, to take charge of her, who commenced at once to treat her, who thought he could ward off the attack. He had ten days the start of the fever, but was not able to arrest the disease which by this time was deeply seated in her system, and on the 7th of October she closed the scenes of this life.

We had now laid away three of our children in the short period of twenty-seven days, and now the fourth one is sick. We had an opportunity to send her away with a friend to the work assigned to me at the recent session of conference, the next day after we buried the third daughter. She was nearly able to ride in a private conveyance to the work, situated forty miles distant. She was at once taken down with a violent attack of the same fever, and for a number of days we thought it would prove fatal. But after being confined for a number of weeks she commenced to recover.

My field of labor this year was the New Goshen circuit, Vigo county, Ind. This work was one of the oldest of the conference and convenient to travel. There were five appointments and these were near each other. Here I had a pleasant year, though not attended with as much success as I desired. My salary this year was $350.

CHAPTER VIII.

In the fall of 1874 the conference was held at Prairieton, Ind. I received for my field of labor this year the Vermillion circuit. This in many respects was a very pleasant year. There were some good revivals on the work and twenty-four accessions to the church. I received this year forty dollars for marrying persons; the most I ever received in one year in this way. My salary was $390. This was an exceedingly wet summer and a large amount of grain was damaged in the shock and stock.

In the fall of 1875 the conference was held at Vermillion, Ill. I was sent to the Long Point circuit. This work comprised of ten appointments situated in the counties of Cumber

land and Jasper. In the winter of this year the
small pox and measles were prevalent on this
work, and in addition to this my health was
poor, so I did but little this year. There were
only six accessions to the church. My salary
this year was $220.

During this year I made my first trip to
the eastern states, taking my family with me.
We started the latter part of July, four of us
in number, and in company with President S.
B. Allen and daughter. The first place we
stopped at was Cleveland, Ohio, Here we remained about twenty hours. The next town
we visited was Buffalo, and from there we went
to Niagara Falls, where spent some over one
day, viewing the scenery of this, the world's
renowned place of visitors. From here we
went to Albany, the capital of the state of New
York. Here we took a steam boat and had a
pleasant ride down the Hudson river to the
city of New York, where we arrived on Saturday. We remained in the city until Tuesday,
when we started to Philadelphia to attend the
great exposition. Here we remained three days
seeing what we could of the centennial show.
From here we went to Baltimore and visited the

Otterbein church and the grave of this great and good man. Here we met old friends among whom was Nehemiah Altman, who used to stop at father's home when I was a boy. In those days he was a peddler but afterward embraced the christian religion and became a successful minister of Christ.

From here we went to Washington where we spent some time in visiting the government buildings and the Smithsonian Institute. We then returned by way of Columbus and stopped several days at Westerville, where we had formerly lived 11 years. Here is where the Otterbein College is located, and where I spent three years and a half, in mental drill, which I have never regretted. Then we stopped awhile at Dayton and visited the Soldiers' Home. We then spent about one week in the bounds of the Miami Conference, on the first field of labor I traveled. We arrived at our home in Illinois some time in September, having enjoyed this trip exceedingly well. On this trip I went to see my mother, who was living with my youngest sister near Richmond, Ind. Salary, $200.

In the fall of 1876 the Conference was held in Middleburg, Clay county, Indiana. From here I was sent to the Richland circuit. This work is located in Shelby county, Illinois. My health was poor, and I was not able to do anything for about four weeks after conference. However I obtained strength sufficient to start to my work which was about fifty miles from home. Here I had a very pleasant year. The Lord blessed us with several good revivals of religion and there were twenty five additions to the church. This made my heart glad to have the evidence that the Lord could use me to lead souls to himself, that he thereby might be honored and glorified. My salary this year was $230.

In May of this conference year the general conference of the church was held at Westfield where my family lived; and where I was permitted to be with them occasioanlly. At this conference we had a very exciting time on the Secrecy question. I was at home during this conference, and enjoyed the privilege of hearing the discussions, and associating with the leading men of the church. This was the third general conference I was permitted to attend. The first was in May, 1853, held at Miltonville, Butter county, O. The second was in May, 1861, at Westerville, Franklin county, O., and the last as I have stated above. But I do not wish to be misunderstood; I was at no time a member of this general assembly. Salary, about $200.

In the fall of 1877 the conference convened at Center Point, Clay county, Ind. Here I was permitted to meet a large number of brethren and sisters with whom I associated the first year of my travel in this conference. How cheering it was to take them by the hand, and look into their friendly faces once more. We had a very pleasant session of conference this year together, and while we were reviewing the past, and contemplating the future, we were inspired with new zeal to go out and work for the Master. O! how cheering and soul inspiring these annual gatherings of the ministers of Jesus Christ are. At the close of this conference at the very time we were having an interesting communion season together, my mother passed away from this troublesome world to to the spirit land, and I shall see her no more until we meet in that better land. She died after an illness of less than half an hour, with heart disease. Although her health was as good as usual, she made a remark that was almost prophetical, early in the morning before she died. Her grand child was an invalid, and her sympathies were stirred in his behalf. The remark was this. "O! John I wish I could take you along with me to heaven to-day."

I received for my field of labor this year the Lawrence circuit, located in Lawrence and Wabash counties. This work was distant about seventy miles from where I lived. It was what is called a good work. There was an abundance of wealth on the work to support a minister and there were plenty of sinners who needed salvation. I met a number on this work with whom I used to associate in Ohio. I stopped with one brother often who used to be at father's home over forty years before. The Lord was with us this year in converting power, We had several good revivals and twenty accessions to the church. My salary this year was $339.

In the fall of 1878 the conference was held at Westfield, Clark county, Ill. At this session

I received the Arthur mission for my field of
labor. A young man with whom I became acquainted during my travels the last year had
some encouragement from members of the
conference that he would receive an appointment to a field of labor at this conference. He
was engaged in the business of teaching school
and had the offer of a school where he lived, but
declined to take it because he expected to enter
upon the active work of the ministry. But at
this conference he failed to get work, which
was a great disappointment to him and he ex-
pressed himself greatly injured financially, as
his opportunity to secure a school had now
passed by.

As we were leaving the conference room he
was telling me his trouble. I at once proposed
to give him my work. He accepted the offer
and the conference ratified the change, and he
traveled the work assigned to me. The preach
er appointed to the Grand Prairie circuit resigned his work and I was appointed to it by the
presiding elder. Things were in a discouraging
condition on this work, and they had been without a preacher for some time. I had some diffi.
culty in getting things arranged properly on

the work. Then there was a church trial to be attended to at once, which was difficult to manage and which effected the work quite a little. But after all we had some success, by way of some conversions and forty-six accessions to the church. I received this year for nine months labor, $140.

In the fall of 1879 the conference was held at Vermillion, Edgar county, Ill. At this conference I was appointed to the Annapolis circuit. It had been a mission the previous year, with an appropriation of twenty dollars. This year two appointments were added, quite a distance from the work—in another county—with only a little financial strength, which paid twenty dollars. I received for compensation this year, eighty-nine dollars; only nine dollars more than the conference paid the preacher missionary money, in addition to what the work paid him. He collected fourteen dollars missionary money on the work, and I collected $14.10. At the end of this year the work was changed to a mission again and received an appropriation.

In the fall of 1880 the conference convened

at Center Point, Clay county, Ind. At this conference I was appointed to the Sullivan circuit, Moultrie county, Ill. This work had paid the preacher but little for a number of years. In 1878 it paid Bro. Cougill but forty dollars, and in 1879 Bro. Rebok's pay was $103. A brother, in view of his wants, received in 1880 $159. So it was apparent I had but little prospect of remuneration. I went however and did the best I could. We had some revival on the work and twelve joined the church. I received a remuneration of $115. I collected for missions eleven dollars. In 1878 nothing was collected for this interest; and in 1879, six dollars were collected. The next year the preacher sent there received three into the church and collected seven dollars missionary money. At the conference of 1881 it was constituted a mission and the preacher received $70 appropriation.

In the fall of 1881 the conference was held in New Goshen, Vigo, county, Ind. At this conference I asked for a location one year. I had taken charge in June of the village paper as its editor. I did this to assist my only son,

Joseph Robert Zeller, to start in this business. He had been working for some time with M. Bair, who was proprietor of this calling in our own. My son was sixteen years of age the 9th of November of this year. We worked together about one year and then when he was a little over sixteen years of age he took charge of the paper as its editor. Although he was so young he gave us a good paper. Indeed some thought it was as good if not better than we had ever before. At an early period in life he embraced religion and joined the U. B. church. He conducted this business only a short time when I induced him to stop this business and go to school.

In the fall of 1882 the conference was held in Parkersburg, Richland county, Ill. At this conference I was appointed to a field of labor composed of a circuit and a mission. There were ten appointments, scattered around in the counties of Jasper, Cumberland and Effingham. After visiting this work and finding the locations of these appointments, I thought: Well, I am spread out entirely too far. I must necessarily be quite thin after this expansion. What in the world do the big men of the conference mean; the bishop and the presiding elders must expect a wonderful amount of work from an old man nearly sixty years of age.

Well, I commenced the work of course under great discouragement. I commenced a protracted meeting the 1st of October. After continuing this meeting about two weeks with considerable success I received word that my boy was dangerously sick. When I arrived at home I found that my boy had been already quite sick ten days, with but little hopes of his recovery. He lingered between life and death for over two weeks longer and died, leaving us but one child living.

While I was attending conference in September before, while in the cornfield getting some feed for the pigs, he was bitten by a large ugly worm on the arm, which caused it to swell badly, and made him exceedingly sick for a time. His mother poulticed it and did for him what she thought would be for the best. In a short time after this a house near us burned, and he got up in the night and worked hard taking things out of the house, and became very warm and heated at this work. I think now that the poison in his blood, and being heated by work was without doubt the cause of his death. He died the 21st day of November, 1882, being 18 years and 12 days old. This was an exceedingly sad time for us all. This was a hard years work for which I received only $130. I had to sell my horse to get the essentials of life to live upon.

This work remained in this way only one year and was separated again. Only a short time before a work was arranged in a similar way to which I was sent. So it was when there was an unpleasant experiment to be made, it was generally my lot to lead out and try it; at least, so it looked to me. We are assured in the bible that all things work together for good to them that love the Lord. These hardships and trials doubtless have their part in the culture and drill necessary to develop our moral character and prepare us for whatever awaits us in this life, and also to purify and refine our characters, through the atoning merits of Christ, for a happy immortality in the world to come.

In the fall of 1883 the conference was held at Westfield, Clark county, Ill. I received as my field of labor the New Goshen circuit. I traveled this work ten years before and was well acquainted with the membership. In that respect it was pleasant. But there had been trouble on the work the year closing, which made it gloomy for me to enter upon my work. The preacher had resigned the work, and it had been without a preacher for three months with the exception of a little work the preacher did for them, who lived on an adjoining work. There were three classes on this field of labor; two of them had some financial strength. One of these was located in the vicinity of the place where the preacher had his trouble the previous year, and this class was left without an organization of officers. I made on effort to have the class elect a leader and steward but this proved a failure. I succeeded in getting a brother to steward part of the class next to him. But there was only a little done at this place during the year; not only was there a failure financially, but it was so largely in other respects. The appointment was continued and I think there was a better state of feeling

at the close of the year. At the other appointments we had good revivals of religion.

I arranged with Bro. H., a minister of a
sister denomination, to assist him at a meeting
in the town of S., where the U. B. had a num
ber of members conveniently located. When I
called on him his meeting had been in session
already about two weeks. I found the good
brother sadly discouraged. He had just closed
a meeting two miles distant with but little success and was about to close this one also. I
said to him: We close our meetings often too
soon. He agreed to continue the meeting if I
would assist him. I said I had come for that
purpose, but I would expect him to help me
in return. This he cheerfully consented to do.
The house in which he was holding the meeting
was a nice one, seated with high back chairs.
They had an organ and a choir. The house
had been built six years, but during this time
had not been blessed with a single conversion.

The first night I talked the pastor did not
invite penitents for prayer. The second night
after I preached I said if there were any who
desired to be christians to come forward and
give me their hand and we would have a short

season of prayer together. A gray headed man sixty-seven years old, in the back part of the house, arose and said: "I am now old and have neglected the interests of my soul. I have often felt that I should be a christian. I believe I will commence the work to-night of living a christian." And as he was speaking the last words he came walking up to me and gave me his hand. During this scene we were favored with the Divine presence and a holy solemnity pervaded the assembly. We had a very clear verification of the promise of Jesus: "Where two or three are gathered together in my name there am I in the midst of them." Inquiring penitents came forward by the dozen and we had one of the most interesting meetings I ever attended. The meeting continued ten days after my connection with it, and resulted in fifty-five conversions who professed faith in Christ and joined the church. This was in many respects a pleasant year but the support was meager.

In the fall of 1884 the conference was held in the village of New Hebron, Crawford county, Ill. I received this year the Arthur mission for my field of labor. I remained on this work three months and received but little remuneration; about enough to meet traveling expenses. I traveled some on the cars and the rest of the time a-foot. I then resigned the work.

At the commencement of the year 1885 I employed to work for the American Bible society and canvassed a large part of Clark county, visiting from house to house. I sold this year about one thousand bibles and testaments. Usually on the Sabbath I preached or lectured on the evidences of christianity, or the inspiration of the scriptures and secured funds for the Bible society.

In the latter part of October of this year I arranged to preach for two Presbyterian churches, located in the southeastern part of this county where I had been working for the bible cause. I remained with these churches until the Spring meeting of the Mattoon Presbytery. I continued to preach for the Presbyterian church one year from this time. I then labored for two other churches; one located in Newton, Jasper county, Ill., and the other ten miles south of this. I was received into the Mattoon Presbytery of this church at Taylorville, Christian county, Ill., the 7th day of April, 1887. So you see I preached for the Presbyterians and had charge of four churches some considerable time before I joined this church.

I have been often asked: " Why did you leave the U. B. church after being a member of it from 1838 to 1887; almost forty-nine years?" Well, there are various influences that led to this change. I left Ohio in 1871. I found that United Brethrenism was different in Illinois from what it was in Ohio. And first permit me to remark, I found the sentiment on infant baptism was almost ignored in practice. Then I became acquainted with a number of U. B. preachers in the west who were strongly. in favor of administering the ordinance of baptism by immersion and were quite Baptist in their sentiments. Then I found I was not in harmony with the great majority on the nature and design of this sacrament. I found that my views were in harmony with the Presbyterians on these subjects. The following is their declaration and formulary on baptism:

Baptism is a sacrament, wherein the wash ing with water in the name of the Father, Son and Holy Spirit, doth signify and seal, our ingrafting into Christ, and partaking of the benefits of the covenant of grace, and our engagement to be the Lord's.

This so perfectly met my views on the nature and design of baptism, that I did not want anything more complete. Then a number of the U. B. Ministers believed in the contingent knowlege of God: this I could not endorse. I never could endorse the policy of many of the U. B. ministers who would compass sea and land to make proselytes, and take them into the church; and a minister's reputation consisted largely in the number of members he could report to the annual conference; when often many they would take in the church, did it more harm than good. Then another objection was to the presiding eldership of the church. There are results which naturally grow out of this system which fosters selfishness and favoritism. It often results in a few, lording it over God's heritage, in a very unpleasant manner. It may be that there is no church government that is perfect. But I believe in the parity of the ministry, and also the right of the Pastor in connection with the other members of the church session, which are ruling elders, to rule and control the church, was the Apostolic method. I can not believe that there was a high official that would come around at stated times to call in question the actions and doings of the pastors. Then lastly the frequent changes of the ministers was a serious objection. Now these are some of the reasons why I changed church relations. I have no ill feelings toward the brethren in the church I left, but wish them abundant success; many of them I know are good men.

In April 1887 I took charge of the Pleasant Prairie church in Coles Co., Ill. I preached for them half time for eleven months. I had a very pleasant time and would have remained longer, but in September of this year engaged to preach for a church in Shelby Co. half of the time; then the brethren of another church in the same county who were connected with this church for years, came to me and insisted on my taking the other church also. I could not without resigning the Pleasant Prairie church, which I did the next spring rather reluctantly. I received ten into the church and baptised four children. I received salary for half the time, eleven months, $250.

I then moved to Tower Hill, Shelby county, Ill., in April, 1888. The other church alluded to was called Prairie Bird. I assisted in holding a meeting at this church in August before. We had a communion season. I took two members into the church on profession. I then had charge or these two churches for two years more, making for the one church three years lacking five months. I also assisted in holding a meeting at Tower Hill the last week in December 1887 before I moved there. I had a pleasant time on this field of labor and the last year I preached for a third church. This charge had been a home mission charge; but it was self supporting while I was with it, and has continued so since. I took 17 members into the church, and received between four and five hundred dollars salary each year. Our only child living, having moved to Westfield where we formerly lived, and Mrs. Zeller in view of this, wishing to go back to our old home, I resigned the charge.

In 1890 I took charge of two churches in Champaign county, Bloomington Presbytery.

The church of Mahomet and one eight miles east. Here 1 made my home and paid my boarding. I had a pleasant year, received $550, salary and received several into the church. I could not remain longer on this work although I was kindly requested to do so. In 1891 I preached for the New Hope church south of Greenup, Jasper county, Ill. In October 1892 I took charge of three churches in the southeastern part of Clark county, Ill. Two of these churches were the first Presbyterians I labored for was in 1885 and 1886.

Erratum: In 4th line, page 117, material should read natural.

END OF PART FIRST.

—THE—

BIOGRAPHY

OF

MARY, ANGIE and LOUISA ZELLER,

Who Died near each other in 1873, with
TYPHOID FEVER.

WITH

Some of Their own Writings

ALSO, A

SKETCH

Of the LIFE of

DANIEL OSCAR ZELLER,

A brother of their's; who died in

1872.

WESTFIELD. ILL.
1881.

CONTENTS.

PREFACE.

In giving the following pages to the public, the writer makes no pretentions to literary ability; for he knows full well, that there are many who will discover errors in this his first effort to publish a work.

The lives of his three children have been so very remarkable in many respects, that it will be interesting to persue these pages, even with their imperfections that may be found in them. Now I trust that these humble pages will accomplish all that the writer had in view in publishing them. And now this little work is dedicated to the children and youth of the U. B. Church.

By the Author, S. W. Zeller.

INTRODUCTION.

In the Summer of 1873, the healthy village of Westfield was visited with the most terrible scourge of typhoid fever that was ever known in this region of Country. Among the many who suffered during this contagion that swept over this stricken village, was the family of the writer of the following pages, three of whose children fell victims to its terrible ravages. I have been impressed for years that something should be written giving items of the lives. and characters of these three girls, who were much loved and respected by those who knew them best. I have concluded to publish a part of their literary productions, they prepared during the two years they were students in Westfield College. And in addition to this, I will include a short sketch of the life of their brother, who preceded them one year and seven months to the better land.

My object in doing this, is, I trust, to accomplish good; and I pray that these pages may be instrumental in awakening, and leading many to love and work more faithfully for the blessed Saviour.

It will be the object of the writer of these pages to give a few plain, unadorned incidents in the lives of four of his chilnren, who, in the providence of God, were called away by the relentless hand of death, at an interesting period of life.

THE EARLY LIFE OF MARY ZELLER.

Mary Elizabeth Zeller, the oldest, was born in Butler County, Ohio, near Indian Creek, about seven miles West of Hamilton, the county seat, on the first day of June, 1850.

She was quite delicate the first months of her life, and the parents had a great anxiety about her, often thinking her days would be few on earth. There was, however, a favorable change. She improved in health and commenced growing rapidly, and at the age of five months was a very interesting and lovely child. At the age of nine months she commenced to walk, and in two weeks she could walk alone with entire freedom. At the age of ten months she was taken with the whooping-cough; this affected her but little, and with the exception of the time she was under the influence of the paroxysms peculiar to this disease, appeard to be in the best of health. Her mother taught her the alphabet, and when but two years old she could name every letter.

In September following her second birthday her father entered upon the work of the itinerant ministry of the church, and being from home for weeks at a time, when he would return she would run to meet him with delight.

When a little past three years of age, her parents left the farm and moved to a village called Millville, on the banks of Indian Creek. Here the United Brethren had a large and flourshing class, and a fine, large brick church house, forty feet wide by 60 long. There she was much interested in attending Sabbath School. Her parents remained at Millville but one year, and then removed to Westerville, Franklin Co. Ohio, where the senior college of the church was located. There were good opportunities for the development of intellect, and moral culture. She was very anxious to learn to read, and was much delighted in going to the district school. She came home one evening sad and gloomy. The cause of this was that she had heard during the day that children under five years of age were in the school unlawfully, and were liable to be dismissed. She ascertained that it was only a short time until she would be five; and said very emphatically to her mother:"If they turn me out of school, you can soon put me in again." Rev. B. R. Hanby, son of ex-Bishop Hanby, who was at that time a student in the College, took a deep intrest in the children of the town. He taught them to sing, and after this for some time was their preacher. She thought very much of Bro. Hanby.

In early life she became interested in religion and in the winter of her twelfth year, made a public profession of religeion and was received into the church at Westerville, Franklin County, Ohio by her own father, who was pastor of the church at that time. When the privilege was given to extend the hand of fellowship to her, Rev. J. M. Spangler, a minister of the conference, came forward with tears in his eyes and gave her his hand. He remarked afterwards: "I could not refrain from shedding tears when little Mary was taken into church by her own father." She was baptized soon after by ex-Bishop Hanby. She dearly loved the means of grace, and had much to say about the good meetings held for the special benefit of the children by B. R. Hanby.

When about thirteen years of age she entered the preparatory department of the College, in which she remained about two years.

In her fifteenth year her parents moved about twenty-three miles from Westerville, to the southern part of the county. There was a wonderfully sad contrast between the place left and the new home. The country was new and the improvements poor, and everything forbidding. Church privileges were quite different here. Instead of preaching twice every Sabbath, now once in three weeks; and instead of Sabbath school every Sabbath morning, now there was none at all. Mary felt very sad and discouraged on acount of these things. She went to her father one morning and said: "Father may I have your horse to ride some to-day?" He asked: "What do you want to do, Mary?" She replied: "I cannot think of living here without a Sabbath school. I want to canvass the neighborhood and see if I cannot raise money enough to start a Sabbath school." I need scarcely say that the father cheerfully gratified her wishes in this respect, and off she started upon her mission. It was not a failure; for in the short time of about one day she raised over thirty dollars for this good enterprise. Now think of it. She was not fifteen years old, being prompted by a love for the Sabbath school, and a desire to do good, started out among strangers and going from house to

house; and none refused to listen to her request,
and but few, if any, who were at all able, but
cheerfully responded to her call by contributing to
this noble enterprise. The school was then organized at once, and a flourishing school it was. From
the influence of this school mainly, during the
early part of the ensuing winter, there was a gracious revival of religion in this place, and a number of accessions to the church. There was one remarkable conversion that should not be omitted
in this narrative, as Mary was the instrument in
the hands of God of her conversion. She was
known and recognized in the community as Dickey Flanders. She was very intelligent and well
educated, and about five years the senior of Mary.
Her family connections and relations in general
were worldly-minded and wicked, and had their
enjoyments in worldly associations and sinful
pleasures. Miss Flanders came to the Sabbath
school and formed the acquaintance of Mary. At
once quite an intimacy grew up between them.
Dickey and Mary were often together on the Sabbath, the former often accompanying the latter
home from school and church; for very soon Miss
Flanders became interested in attending the preach-

ing of the word of God as well as the Sabbath school; and, indeed, there is such a similarity between these two means of grace that it would be difficult to hold to the one and despise the other. In an effort made directly for the conversion of persons, Miss F. was awakened, and made the subject of Gods's renewing grace. I shall never forget this interesting occasion. Persons are seldom more deeply penitent and more earnest seekers of salvation than was this lady, and the effort was not in vain. The good seed had been sown in the Sabbath school, and it produced the happy fruit of love to God and a consecrated life to his service. Miss F. lived a faithful christian life, and died a happy death some years after.

Before Mary was fifteen years of age she obtained, at Columbus, O., a certificate to teach school. The examinations at this time were oral, and it was near the middle of the day when she entered the room where the public examination was held; there was a board of three who conducted the examination: each had a class busily engaged at work when she entered the room. She was invited to take a seat in a class with other teachers, and after answering questions quite sat-

isfactorily for about an hour. this examiner reported to his associates that Mary was quite worthy of
a certificate; it was made out and given to her,
while about twenty who were in the classes when
she entered were retained when she left the room.

She completed the most of her first term of
teaching before she was sixteen, and rendered good
satisfaction to the district.

In the Spring of the year after her sixteenth
birthday, she took the train at Columbus, Ohio
went to Hamilton, and spent two or three months
among relatives in the Miami Valley, and returned
home another way to where her father had moved during her absence, near the city of Lancaster,
Fairfield Co., Ohio, making this trip of over three
hundred miles alone, without a single person being with her with whom she was in the least acquainted.   This trip, requiring a number of
changes, was made without any dificulty: a little
more than the most of girls of her age would undertake.

She was at home only a short time, until,
through her earnest solicitations, her father permitted her to go into the millinery business in the
city of Lancaster, not however, without having se-

rious impressions, and plainly telling her of the probable unfavorable results of this business to her health. But she was not satisfied unless she was in some occupation by which she could assist her father in bearing a part of the expenses of the somewhat large family. While in this business, for about four years, she formed many acquaintances, and had many warm friends who loved her dearly, and who often spoke decidedly in her favor; but she was loved and honored mostly, while in the city, for her piety and devotion to the Sabbath school. As an evidence of the esteem the church had for her, she received from its members a beautiful certificate of life membership in the Missionary Society. During the time of her father's residence in the city of Lancaster, which was nearly three years, she would sometimes accompany him to his fields of labor, and assist him in protracted meetings. One meeting will never be forgotten by her father. This was when she was about eighteen years of age. After the meeting had been in session a few days, there was a direct appeal made to the unconverted to at once consecrate themselves to the Lord Jesus and his blessed cause by coming forward to the alter of prayer.

Mary went out through the congregation and plead with sinners to accept the call, and be reconciled to the Savior. Many were persuaded by her to come forward to the altar of prayer, and while they were kneeling there, were happily converted. How exceedingly she rejoiced to see sinners converted, and made happy in the Savior's love. This was a blessed meeting, and the result largely of Mary's faithful labors. Oh! my young friends, how much good you could accomplish if you were consecrated workers for Christ. Young persons, if truly pious, will have an influence with persons of their age that older persons cannot have.

In the summer of 1871, she emigrated with her parents to Westfield, Clark County, Ill. There she was admitted as a student in the College about the first of September, and continued in school the most of the time until her death. Soon after her arrival at Westfield she was selected by the Supt., Prof. W. R. Shuey as a teacher of the Sabbath school. This position she filled with promptness and honor, being much esteemed by the members of her class, and this relation she sustained to the school when called away to her reward in Heaven. How blessed it is to be engaged

in so good a work when the Master comes to call
us home.

In the Spring of 1873 she was engaged to teach
school about three miles southwest of town, in
the Goble neighborhood. Here she succeeded a-
gain, as she did in almost every thing she under-
took.

She was stricken down with the typhoid fever
on the tenth day of September, 1873, after suffering intensely for about fifteen days. She frequently said during her affliction that she would not
get well again, but would surely die. A cloud of
temptations and gloom settled down upon her
mind during the early part of her affliction. She
spoke of her unworthiness; but the clouds gave
way, and the presence of the blessed Jesus was
precious, and spoke of her prospects of a home in
the better land. She said to her father the day
before her death: "I am going soon to leave you,
and I want to tell you while I have the ability to
talk; I may not be able to converse with you
when I come to die. I wish you would tell all my
friends to meet me in Heaven." Was not this a
presentment by her kind Father in Heaven of her
condition in a dying hour, for it proved true to

the letter in her case.

The last conversation her father had with her a short time before the last struggle came, she said: "I am passing away; the shadow is gathering round me. I cannot see." The indications were that she would live but a few hours. A little past four o'clock on the sad day, death came to her relief, and she passed to a far better and happier clime. Although the day was clear and bright, during her struggle in death, there was for a time a light above the brightness of day around her face as she passed away. The funeral services were conducted by Rev. Wm. McGinnis, who was pastor of the charge, and Rev. ☀ B. Allen, President of the College. Her body was then laid away to rest quietly until the resurrection morn; while her spirit doubtless is mingling with the pure ones around the throne of God in the better land.

BIOGRAPHY OF MARY AND ANGIE·

When I mention the name of Mary F. and S.A. Zeller many of our readers, familiar with these names, will pause and inquire, "What of them? what of Mary and Angie?" My reply must be,"Much that is sad." Yet there is much that is sweet, much admirable, everything honorable, every thing of good report. The sad part is that they have both died. I thought when Mary was gone that the rent in family, church, and social circle was far too large; but soon—in only three days—Angie was gone too, and "the mourners went about the streets"—ay, the streets were full of mourners.

Mary. Zeller died September 11th, 1873, aged 23 years 3 months and 10 days. S. Angeline Zeller died September 14th, 1873, aged 21 years and 3 days.

Thus their brief day of life is closed, their night of death has come; and as they were wont to lie side by side upon their nightly couch beneath their father's roof, they are now lying side by side in "the house appointed for all living." In life, as true, loving sisters, they were ever companions of each other, and in death they are not separated

Typhoid fever, that defier of medical skill, seized upon them and, after a painful and protracted struggle, proved victor, and they faded away from our midst.

Rarely is it necessary to chronicle so serious a loss. True there is no period when friends can feel that it is a fit time to lose a friend. A civilized household ever craves more and more of the association of all its members— the infantile, the youthful, the mature, and the old None can be spared. We refuse to death the right of way to any heart we love. But when, of all ages, could he rob us worse than when he carries of the blooming son or daughter, whose steps are just at the threshold of maturity; talented, too, and educated, and skilled for usefulness, and amiable in spirit? Such a seizure has he made from the household of our dear brother, Rev. S. W. Zeller; and that seizure too, as we have seen, is a double one. If "one had been taken and the other left," it would have been indeed hard to bear; but when we reflect that both are taken, that father and mother became objects of our deepest sympathy and our most earnest prayers. Oh, may this terrible experience prove a purifying fire to gloriously refine and beautify their hearts, long ago bent to the gospel yoke! May divine grace, which has enabled them to pass through this ordeal without one word of discontent, so inflate their souls as to ever keep them aloft above the storms of life—spiritual aeronauts above the clouds. But not only parents are sufferers. Hearts of brother, sisters, and tenderly loving companions have been absolved by this regretted stroke.

Both these sisters are recorded among the recent students of Westfield College. Both had made high marks in the intellectual struggle, so as to be an honor both to their family and the college. High hopes were justly indulged in by the parents and instructors, and by all who were estimating the rising forces of the Church—hopes that these lights, after a little more trimming by the hand of education, would do much to dispel the darkness of earth.

Already had their influence been felt, strongly felt, as co-workers with other servents of Christ. Quite early in life they gave themselves to Jesus Christ. Idlers in the vinyard they were not. They "had not so learned of Christ." well had they heeded the divine injunction, 'whatsoever thy hand findeth to do, do it with thy might.' Accordingly, their connection with Christianity was not a merly nominal one as regards good works.

Years ago, Mary (little Mary then) was one of the precious few whose piety did not wane with the winter moons The writer, together with others of "class No. 3," in the church at Westerville, Ohio, can well recollect the exemplary regularity and consistency of her childhood life. It will be a pleasure to all those classmates who are yet surviving, to learn that the buds which then so beautifull adorned her young character were not blasted, but continued fruiting untill the frost of death so untimely cudown the plant. To these classmates, and to all her friends, she left a message. Many hours before her death she said, as if prophetically, 'When I am dying I shall not be able to speak; therefore I want you, father, to tell all my friends to meet me in heaven." As she expected, her speech was gone long before her trial ended. Bodily, her dying-bed was not as soft and downy pillows: it was hard; and for a time it seemed as if she must pass away without a sign of her inward state. But just at the last moment, just when cruel Death, after racking her frame in a convulsive struggle, had apparently completed his work and ceased, her face, from writhing in a spasm, instantly became wreathed in a heavenly smile that plainly showed the victory and the joy within.

Sometimes days of cloud, and rain, and storm, days gloomy and forbidding, are illuminated at evening by an outburst of brightest sunshine from behind the western blackness; and then we are all made glad. So it seemed in the death of Mary Zeller. Her dying smile asserted, with delightful plainness, that her agonies were only of the body, and that her soul was bursting out with the new wine of heaven. Let us heed her admonition and meet her in that bright land.

Angie embraced religion at fourteen years of age, under the labors of Rev. B. H. Kerns, of the Scioto Conference of the United Brethren Church. For seven years she lived to demonstrate the soundness of her conversion and the strength of her Christian character.

Her last sickness was long and painful; but, like her sister, she "possessed her soul in patience," nor in aught murmured at her lot. While not disguising her hope of recovery, she nevertheless recognized the chances of the opposite, and unhesitatingly and earnestly said, "I want the will of God to be done; I want no will but his."

To her father, whose labors and sacrifices in the service of God have been abundant, as is known to many, she left this dying expression: "Pa, I want you not to quit preaching." As if she feared his manifold trials might overcome him, and lead him to give up his heavenly mission, her spirit, with its vision cleared from sordid mists, was prompted to urge him on in his efforts to rescue men from sin and ruin. He will not forget these words, They will support him in future trials. They will reinvigorate all his purposes as a minister. They will incite him to unprecedented devotion to his calling. Would that all toilers in God's vinyard could always have domestic voices, not only of the dying, but of the living, encouraging them in their toil. With such aids, many a minister's usefulness as well as his comfort, would be more than double.

But Angie's voice can no longer plead for the cause of God. Hushed in silence, her words are all said. How happy that she spoke so many right things! Bound in icy fetters, her feet can no longer run. How good that they were wont to run on errands of mercy! Contrary to her expectations, her work on earth is done. How blessed that she "worked while the day lasted."

It is sad to think that so much of worth, so much of talent, so much of youthful education, so much of loveliness and amiability as abode in these two lost ones should be absolutely buried away from earth. The wise will learn lessons from these sad thoughts; and thus beauty may spring up out of the ashes of our sisters.

SAMUEL B. ALLEN.

Westfield, Ill., September 17, 1873

I; MEMORIAM.

WHEREAS, Our kind and merciful Father has seen fit in his wise and good though sad and mysterious providence to send the death-angel once again into the Philalethean Literary Society of Westfield College, and call from earth to a blissful home in the fair clime of heaven one of its most devoted and best beloved members, Miss Mary E. Zeller, of Westfield, Ill.; and *Whereas*, We deem it fitting that we give public expression to our sorrow and irreparable loss in the death of our sister; therefore,

Resolved. 1. That in the sad and unexpected dispensation we witness the divine hand of our loving Father, and desire, meekly, to bow in submission to his will; that we truly feel that the tender cord of affection unites our hearts with those of bereaved; and we would lovingly mingle our tears with their's in this dark hour of sorrow; yet resting in the assurance that "behind the clouds the sun is still shining," the sun of his love who doeth all things well. who wounds to heal, who has gone to prepare a place for those who love him, where severed cords will be reunited, and where he will wipe all tears from their eyes.

2. That we will ever sacredly cherish her memory, brightened by so many fond recollections, and will strive to live each day in the faith of the holy religion which she so truly honored and exemplified in her life, and through which she so gloriously triumphed in her death.

3. That we wear the usual badge of mourning thirty days.

4. That copies of these resolutions be presented to the bereaved ones; that they be recorded in the journal of our society; and that copies be sent for publication to the RELIGIOUS TELESCOPE, *Clark County Herald. Marshall Messenger, Charleston Plaindealer, Ohio State Journal, Lancaster Gazette, and Westerville Banner.*

DORA F. BOLTON, ⎫
MOLLIE E. ROSS, ⎬ Com.
MATTIE DAVES, ⎭

Philalethean Hall, September 10, 1873.

We will now give our readers some of Mary Elizabeth's productions she prepared while in College only a few months before she died. Written in 1872 and 1873.

IMPROVEMENT OF TIME.

When we look around us and see how uncertain life is and with what velocity time is speeding us on, are we not truly made to feel that the few days, or perhaps years of our mortal existence cannot be too well improved?

Although we commence to lisp the Savior's name at our Mother's knee and unswervingly devote all our lives to His service, and at the same time receive the first principles of mental development, and then industriously and earnestly, we will scarcely ever feel that our time has been as well improved as it could have been. We can look back upon the past to some time, yes indeed many times, in which we might have made more rapid progress.

But the past cannot be reclaimed, and it is useless for us to tarry, longer than learn lessons of warning, which many serve for future aid, in recalling past failures: the present, and only the present is ours, and it is not only a privilege we have but a duty we owe, to ourselves, to our associates, and our Heavenly Father, that we now improve each moment in the best possible manner.

We are now fitting ourselves to enter the great school of eternity, surely we do not have this important truth properly fixed upon our memory or we would not be so sluggish and indifferent, we would find little or no time to spend in adorning the body, in useless and frivolous conversation, in restlessly roaming about in order to destroy time, as we often hear the thoughtless and indolent express themselves.

We would have no time to discuss our neighbors extravagant wardrobe or shabby coat, his false

airs or sedate manner, his complection or imper-
fect features, but if we would seek to aid in eradi-
cating all evil, lend a helping hand to the destitute, and a cheering word to the disconsolate. If
we were thus actively engaged how little dissen-
tion and strife there would be. We would certainly have a paradise on earth, and would be
more fully fitted and qualified for the paradise of
a never ending eternity.

RECOLLECTIONS OF EARLY LIFE.

Memory calls us away from monotinous routine
of school life, to the almost forgotten past. We
are first hastened to the place where we obtained
our first mental and morol instructions. The
means employed, the manner in which those lessons were imparted and the enstructors are all in
view. The little a-b-c tin plate that was studied
principally at meal time. The finger marks in the
frost and steam upon the window pane, in the
form of names, sums and pictures, altegather
making an attractive picture.

Our first with many succeeding school day, our
innumerable trials and difficulties alternating with

sunshine and happiness.

And what tender recollections cluster around the first prayer we learned to repeat. when too young to even know the meaning of prayer and assumed the form simply because Mother said it was right; but still more precious is the time when we laid aside the form and asked our Heavenly Parent to fill our hearts with true devotion.

How signally benificial, although not so pleasant, to recall the dark and stormy part of our history, which assists us in fortifying ourselves against the furious gale which is liable to sweep across our pathway when least expected.

Whether our life has been tempest-tossed or comparatively calm, we love to occasionally review by-gone days.

THE WEEDS OF SIN DEEPLY ROOTED.

Some weeks since, my mind was quite visably impressed that our yard ought to be cleaned.

It being so much larger than the ones I had previously been accustomed to sweep, and owing to the temperature of the weather I was loth to undertake so much. But knowing that weeds would not uprooted themselves but were becoming larger and stronger each day; and the chips, shavings and rubbish were rapidly smothering the tender grass, giving the yard such a wild and deserted appearance, that I at once procured hoe, rake, broom and basket and commenced the work. Economy suggested that I first clean off the weeds. I thought this quite reasonable and proceeded to hoe off the weeds in rapid succession. But imagine, if you like, my chagrin as Ma tapped me upon the shoulder and exclaimed "how stupid," "your plan will do if you desire to repeat this process in a short time; but allow me to suggest that you take these weeds out by roots and you will not need to be annoyed by their appearance again."

I then laid my hoe aside and did as instructed, although some were so well fortified that it required a good degree of strength to remove them. I felt more than repaid for my labor, to know that these weeds could not reappear, also thinking that the greater part of my task was completed.

I then proceded to gather the chips, shavings and small particles from the sod, but I soon found that the most tedious and irksome part was yet

to do. I tried to rake them together into heaps
but either the rake was too large or the chips were
too small and many remained in the grass undis-
turbed.

Finally I found it necessary to sweep the grass,
which took great care and perseverance: but the
agreeable change which this process produced,
more than repaid me for my labor.

Likewise we find the character of persons in
which are large and deeply-rooted weeds of vice,
choking out all good purposes and impressions.
Also the chips. shavings and smaller partiles of
sin leaving no opportunity for the development
of tender loving thoughts and acts of kindness.

Many have been brought to see the rude appearance of their characters; and desiring to sustain, at least. a good reputation, undertake to
remove its rubbish. They proceed to hide from
public view their most aggravating and prominent faults. only cropping off that which can be
seen while the roots are left firm in their natures.

Those who are prudent will endeavor to pluck
their errors up by the roots, although the work
may be difficult and require all the strength they
possess, that they may not shoot forth in some

unguarded moment and cause farther pain.

The smaller faults like the chips and shavings require still more careful attention and persevering energy. and it should be ambition of each individual to toil on until even the dust of immorality is removed. Then his character will sparkle like the pure grass bathed in morning dew.

DECISION AND PERSEVERANCE.

From a want of persevering resolution, and firmness of purpose many fail to make a good record upon time's pages.

Like birds that desert our forests as soon as the chilling winds of autumn appear, some men are prompted to seek other employment when met by opposition and discouragement; or if their occupations do not afford the desired ease, their courage is shaken and they seek fairer climes hoping to acquire a living by less labor and fewer interruptions. But they find difficulties in each pursuit they undertake; and spend more of their time and strength in devising plans to get out of the reach of life's duties than would be required to perform them.

We have the example of one who is apparently less favored. He is poor, and has few friends, but he possesses a decisive and persevering aim to succeed; he asks for the sympathy of no one; realizing that there is work for him to perform, and that he only can steer his barque safely into harbor. The sea is sometimes tempest-tossed, but he moves steadily onward, gaining new strength, and new power over the contending elements. Decision is moulded in his character, and he rows manfully against the current until he reaches the port of happy anticipations.

Not only do individuals incur their own misfortune and unhappiness by an irresolute and unreliable disposition, but often bring sorrow upon those with whom they associate.

The fond Mother is often grieved at the fickle and undecided course of her daughter who is controlled altogether by circumstances, and makes no effort to shape her own future welfare. Domestic duties are too rude for her fastidious taste; and education requires more will and nerve-power than she can command; not because she is destitute of sufficient health and original intellect, but of resolution and perseverance. How much more valuable an object that is procured by sacrifices and earnest labor!

The miner deprives himself of the comforts and many pleasant associations of home, and seeks his fortune in a distant land. He toils many weary days without remuneration, but he has "put his hand to the plow" and does not question whether to cease the pursuit or not. He has invested all in this enterprise, and must now search until the desired treasure is obtained or all his work shall be in vain.

Many fields are yet uncultivated. There is work for all to do; and we are held accountable for the manner in which each moment is employed. Then should we not endeavor to dispell this lethargy that bedims our metal and moral horizon? If we earnestly employ the means within our reach, we shall realize that "A cloudy morning oft brings a pleasant day."

BEHIND THE CLOUDS THE SUN IS STILL SHINING.

When the heavens have been darkened by dense vapor and gathering storms hover o'er for many days, at times lashing the earth in fits of fury, how often we wish for the illuminating splendor of golden sunshine.

We become weary and downcast when the rays of the sun are obstructed from our view by the clouds; the birds cease to trill their sweet notes, and all nature appears dreary and dreamy. But who, being acquainted with her laws would say "give me all sunshine; allow no angry clouds or yet lighter mists to intervene between me and the azure sky?" Not one; for the earth has only been favored with one of her necessary elements. To her, new life has been imparted and when the clouds are dispersed the sun is still sitting on his majestic throne, sending out the rays of his imperial grandeur; and now the earth is prepared to welcome his bright and cheering smiles; the hum of the busy bee is again heard; the warbling of joyous birds appear more melodeous, and our whole being is filled with new vigor and delight.

Thus we find life alternating in clouds and sunshine; none are free from sorrow and affliction. Many are their shades and dimentions; varying like the light and airy clouds that float in etherial brightness to the black and sweeping blast that envelops the whole heavens. We would gladly escape all pain, privation and disappointments; but, what "blessings in disguise!" Were we not sometimes afflicted both mentally and physically how indifferent to each others interests would we become.

Until we have suffered the pangs of disease, had high hopes and aspirations crushed to the earth, and laid dear friends beneath the sod, we are not prepared to sympathize with those undergoing like sorrows. Our hearts are melted to softness; made more flexible by trouble and lifted to the sunlight beyond.

When the clouds are thickest and storms are raging we are apt to murmur, or at least wish the sun would again appear; forgetting that behind them all, he is still performing his great and wonderful mission. Also when we are attacked by mental distress, when some has filled our bosom almost to overflowing, and hope is about yielding to helpless despair, we often think that God's smiles have been transformed into displeasure. But the Eternal Sun of Glory is surely sending out rays of beaming love as if all were light and gladness.

Then take courage when daylight is bedimed and our sky is o'ercast; and banish oll fears; since "Behind the clouds the sun is still shining".

A Contented Mind.

Those who have a contented mind are in possession of a great treasure.

All may enjoy it if they will. Observation teaches us that this precious gem is not always to be found clasping hands with affluence and luxury.

There are many persons who seemingly have

all they desire; but become acquainted with them, or learn a little of their history and you will very soon change your opinion. They prove to be unhappy, and dissatisfied. Always wishing for something beyond their reach, which if they did possess would not help to satisfy their restless, covetous dispositions. For ere one selfish desire could be obtained, there would be others to take its place.

We may have a great many friends, occupying prominent positions in society and possess wealth, but unless we are resigned to the Will of our Heavenly Father, and also willing to improve our time and talents as much as possible, we cannot enjoy the comforts of a contented mind.

Monarchical compared with Republican form of Government.

Government is a systematic arrangement for the exercise of power and authority, over the actions of men, for the purpose of promoting the wellfare of both ruler and subjects.

In order that we may judge of the comparative

merits and demerits of the two forms of Government under discussion, we have but to examine the nature and out croppings of each.

A monarchical form of Government is based upon a sandy foundation; one of man's own selfish devising. How then can it meet the wants of a people who are bound with fetters of serveility; which brings the masses into subjection to one, and must recognize only a favored few as having the rights of free will and free speech; robbing men of the ambition, intellect, and power alloted them by the one great Monarch.

The motives to industry are few. A man who must give the half or three fourths of the products of his labor to sustain the nobility will soon loose all energy, if he even had any, to gain positions of dignity and usefulness. There is nothing to stimulate his weary brain and nerves, and he drops down into dispair, poverty and degredation.

Schools and Colleges are comparativly few, and only those of honorable birth and wealth are able to enjoy their benefits.

In a sentence ignorance, crime and blood-shed are its greatest products.

Not so with a free Republican government: it

is founded upon principals of justice and "good-will toward all men." It coincides with Holy Writ, and is the only sure road to peace and prosperity.

How innumerable are the pleasures and enjoyments of our beloved America to-day? Whence come all these blessings? We answer by complying with the demands of equity.

"TRIBULATION AN AGENCY FOR GOOD."

If we notice the etymology of the word "tribulation," which is derived from the latin word "tribulum," this word signifying a threshing instrument, which was used in ancient times by the Romans for separating the corn from the husk, we can understand better its true meaning.

I will attempt to show that tribulation is a means for separating the evil in the world from the good.

It seems to be one of the many ways by which God establishes good among mankind: and I think deserves not to be omitted or passed by as not belonging to this class: if we attempt to prove this statement, history will not leave us without aid. Its pages contain many instances in which good has been brought out of evil, and joy out of sorrow. It has often been of great value when no other power could turn a people from their evil ways; when they seemed to think that they were their own masters, and no other nation had a right to dictate to them what they ought to do; and how they should conduct their ways: and although they were determined to continue to do as they had done: yet when the chastening rod of affliction was laid upon them, when they were brought to feel their dependence by some pestilence or famine, they were willing and ready to listen to and accept the advice of others, to review their past actions, see where they had done wrong and endeavor to do better.

It was in the furnace of affliction that God prepared his children in Egypt for doing the good which they afterwards accomplished.

And the same might be said about the founders of our country. They were prepared for this noble work in England, while undergoing persecutions from their neighbors, none of which they deserved, but which they endured for the sake of their religion. Their persecutors knew but little about what they were doing, when they drove them out from among them: and yet no doubt they fulfilled their Creators design in compelling them to form a new state and, organize a new and free government. If these persons had been well treated in their former country, it is doubtful whether they ever would have made an effort to do anything except for their own enjoyments, or ever have done the good which they did under these circumstances.

It is the nature of the whole human family to sink into a state of quietude and ease, caring only for their own wellfare, and never attempting to do anything for any person else, or for the good of their country, unless aroused to action by some threatening voice, or fearful calamity. "Each one for himself:" is the general motto and instead of helping a neighbor on over the rough road of life. Each does all he can to pull him back; instead of clearing his way, he heaps up brush to make it as rough as he can, instead of being his friend, he is his enemy.

We may also see how tribulation has been the means of furnishing us many writings of great value. John Bunyan wrote his "Immortal Allegory" in Bedford jail where he was confined for several years, for preaching the gospel in an unauthorized manner. He refers to this when he speaks of the "Den." "The Lord often causes the wrath of man to praise him." Had Bunyan not been shut up in jail it is not probable that we should ever have seen the Pilgrims Progress.

And not only this has been left through the means of affliction to bless the world, but many other writings which doubtless would never have been composed had they not been done under circumstances of affliction.

With what pride does the farmer look upon his fields of grain ripe and for harvest when not half of their worth can be seen, for before the rich and useful flour appears, the chaff and weeds must be separated from that wheat. And this is enough, but the grains must even be torn in pieces by the mill: then we may see its true worth pure and refined. So it is with man. If he is good and noble, and if he is in possession of all those principles which would characterize a man of worth, yet his true value will not be estimated so highly, as after his person has been touched by affliction.

He is like the wheat in the straw. The flails of God's corrections must be laid upon him, and all those rain thoughts and desires of his threshed away. The dust and chaff of the world must be separated from him. Then he is prepared to seek for those treasures the most noble and lasting.

How many of us, after being released from the chamber of the sick and suffering, have not realized that we were better than before we entered?

While there, how many good resolves did we make? and how many plans did we lay for doing better in the future, which we afterwards followed?

In a place like this we are among solemn realities, the mind being shut in from the world and all.

BIOGRAPHY.

SARAH ANGELINE ZELLER.

Sarah Angeline Zeller, the second in age, was born September 11th, 1852, near the same place where her older sister was, as already stated. She grew up very much as children usually do who are favored with religious influences. She accompanied her older sister to Sabbath school when quite young, and in this enjoyed herself quite well in the early part of life. As soon as she was old enough she attended district school, and in this succeeded quite well. When nine years of age, in connection with her older sister, she took lessons in instrumental music. Here she showed more than ordinary ability, and soon surpassed others of riper years.

When fourteen years of age she had a serious attack of congestive fever. This was in the fall of 1864. It was exceedingly wet, and rained a great deal. The streams became very much swollen. I was attending the annual conference, which convened that year in Vinton County, Ohio. The rain and swollen streams kept me from returning home for nearly a week after the close of the conference. In my absence, Angie, as she was familiarly called, was taken sick. As soon as I returned home I called a physician, who did all he could for her relief. After she had been confined to her bed for about four days, the whole family were much startled by her impressive talk about dying. She called her mother to her bedside, and said: "O, mother, I heard the angels sing so beautifully. And the blessed Jesus came and took all my pain away. I will not stay in this world any longer. O. mother, I will go up an l live with the blessed Jesus and with the beautiful angels. Now mother I am going to die. I want you to bury me at Westerville, beside my little brother." Her brother, about four months old, died eight years before. She often visited the village cemetery, and assisted her sister to plant beautiful flowers on his little grave. Her mother was so much affected that it was much easier for her to cry than to talk with her dying child, as she then thought. She kept on insisting for this until her mother was able to gratify her with an affirmative answer, which entirely satisfied her. But now she has another request to make that interests her not a little.

She says; "Mother, I do not think it is nice when one is dead to lay them out on a board. Please let me lay on the bed until you get ready to bury me."

This being granted, she was soon resting quietly, without any suffering or pain at all. What she had said appeared to be true to the letter; her pain was all gone, and it was so sudenly removed, almost in a moment. Was she not right in supposing that the blessed Savior came and removed all her pain? Having been at one of the neighbors for a few minutes during this exciting talk of hers, a messenger was sent, met me half way on my return home, and said, "Angie is dying." As soon as possible I was by her bedside, and while she was lying quietly and comfortably, the family were shedding tears of sorrow, as much so as if she were dead. As I inquired of her how she felt, she repeated to me the most of what she had said to her mother, about the angles singing, and what Jesus did for her. I cannot describe to you my feelings in this hour; it is a mingling of joy and sadness; sadness because we thought in all probability she would soon leave us: joy because she was so joyful and happy in anticipation of realizing so soon a happy home with Jesus and the angles. Several of the neighbors came in and kindly rendered us all the assistance they could. I shall never forget them; they thought she would surely die. After the excitement had subsided, I took a chair and sat down by the side of my companion, and conversed with her about the probable result of the strange scene, and we concluded she would die, and we made some arrangement for the inter-

ment of her body as she had requested to be done.
After this I went to her bedside, and found her
resting as quietly and sleeping as sweetly as she
ever did in her life. She was lying with her face
from me, next to the wall of the room. I spoke to
her tenderly, and she turned over and looked me
full in the face. I had prepared some medicine the
doctor had left for her. I said: "Angie, here is
some medicine I want you to take." "No," she replied rather emphatically: "I am not going to stay
in this world, I am not going to take any more
medicine either." I insisted on her taking it, but
she refused, and this was the first time she objected in the least to take what we thought would be
good for her. One of the neighbors present thought
I had better not insist on her taking it, so she had
it her own way. By the next day she had so far
recovered that she was able to sit up in a chair,
and in a very short time was in her usual health.
I believe the Lord Jesus appeared to her in mercy
during this affliction, and not only relieved her of
bodily pain, but also imparted to her the comforts
of religion; and if called away at this time she
would, without a doubt, have gone to the better
land. She was a good child and had a mild and ge-

- nial nature. She attended school at the Otterbein College in the fall and winter of the same year
In the latter part of the winter of this year, she returned home, and at a meeting held by Rev. B.
H. Kearns, in the southern part of Franklin Co.,
Ohio, she made a public profession of religion,
and united with the church; and ever after was an
active christian. When in her sixteenth year she
entered the graded schools in the city of Lancaster,
and here she had an opportunity, under the tuition
of an eminent musician, to cultivate her musical
talent. She was much delighted with music, and,
when not otherwise engaged would sing and play
on the piano. She enjoyed herself very much in
this way; and was always happy to entertain her
friends with impressive instrumental music. She
was not only interesting and attractive in the
parlor, but eminently so in the kitchen. There
never was a more industrious and faithful person,
ready to do anything in or about the house that
was needful to be done. It was a common thing
for her, while attending school, when she returned from the recitation room, to go immediately to
the kitchen and inquire of her mother if she
could do anything for her.

She had many warm friends in Ohio, especially is this true of many with whom she became acquainted while living in the city of Lancaster. In the summer of 1871 she entered college classes in Westfield, Clark Co., Ill. In this place the remainder of her short and eventful life was spent. She lacked but one year of completing the ladies' course in this College.

Soon after her arrival in Westfield she was selected by the Sabbath school Supt., W. R. Shuey, as one of the Sabbath school teachers, which office she filled during the remainder of her life. In the winter previous to her death, during a revival of religion, she was at least in part, instrumental in the conversion of all the scholars of her class.

How very pleasant it was to have these call and visit her during her last sickness, and this they did quite often. Angie was very modest and unassuming, and was an example of piety, and devoted to the cause of religion. She had obtained, by faithful labor, a good education, was well drilled in the sciences and also in music. This enabled her to contribute largely, in the social circle, to the cheer and happiness of all around her. While she is doubtless missed in other places, her absence is most seriously felt in the family by father and mother, brother and sister. She was taken with the typhoid fever on the thirteenth of August, 1873, and after suffering intensely for thirty-two days, death came to her relief. Three days before she died she said to me in a plain, clear voice: "Will you please get me the almanac?" I did so. She turned to the month of September and said: "To-day I am twenty-one years old." I replied, "Yes, you are now your own girl, but we will keep you yet awhile." She looked at me significantly and said not a word. I then had a good deal of encouragement that she would get well; but alas! how soon this hope was torn from me.

One incident I must not forget to relate. During the time we were in Illinois, our expenses were large, and my salaray small. This made it discouraging, not only to myself, but also to the family, and Angie sympathized with me in this difficulty; and fearing I would turn aside from the ministry and engage in some more lucrative calling, she said to me while on her dying bed: "Now father, I don't want you to leave the ministry. I think it is your duty to declare the blessed gospel of salvation to men. Continue on in this good work." While that matter was settled between myself and my Father in heaven, years before, still this earnest request of hers affords me real comfort amidst the dark hours of temptation through which I am called to pass so often in this life.

Her sister Mary was taken away from us three days and a half before she left us. For several weeks it was thought Angie would go first; but as time rolled on Mary declined very rapidly and died first. We were then more anxious than ever in behalf of the remaining sick one, who had suffered so long and patiently. But now there were new difficulties before us. Angie knew nothing of the death of her sister, and it was a very difficult matter to determine whether to let her know it or not, in her very feeble condition.

After consulting with the family and a few friends of the family on this subject, we determined to inform her of this matter. As I was carefully laboring to introduce this matter, she at once comprehended the condition of things and remarked; "O, is Mary dead?" I answered in the affirmative. Tears gathered in her eyes and ran down her cheeks, but she was not very much excited. but said: "You must bring her in and let me see her before you bury her." This we did, and she looked upon her perhaps half a minute. She said nothing about her sister after this until the night she died, when she appeared to have an interesting conversation with her. She called her by name, beckoning with her hand, and asking her to come to her. She described to her how she was dressed, all the particulars, even better than could have been done by those who did the work. This is evidence that the mind is independent of the body, and exists when the body is cold and silent in death; for this exercise of intellect was just a short time before the spirit left the body.

I will now allude to two impressive dreams that our pastor, Rev. Wm. McGinnis, had, the one before and the other during our sad afflictions. He thought in his dream that the two sisters, Mary and Angie, and himself were walking together in the country, and they came to where the timber was all cut off, and the white stumps made an impressive appearance. He said to them, "What is this?" "O," said they, "this is Pa's clearing," and all at once Angie became very sick and fainted, and it was with difficulty that they returned home again. How true and sad this was verified. It was verily a clearing, for in a short time of twenty-six days the three oldest of the family were taken away from us. About two days after the death of Mary, he had another impressive dream. He thought a number of our family and himself were riding in a carriage and he was driving a very large, fine-looking horse; they came to an elevation in the road that was perpendicular and exceedingly high, and when they came to this place the horse commenced at once to ascend this steep, and when partly up, he stepped out of the carriage, handed the lines to those within, and looked after them until they had gone up over the hill far away to the plains beyond. I anxiously inquired of him, how many were in the carriage: The answer was indefinite. It may be that the dream was of the same nature. Ah! yes, here was the great dark horse of Death, bearing many of the family over the hill, upon the plains of Eternal life.

I will give the reader some of Sarah Angie Zeller's productions while she attended school.

No place like home.

We may mingle, in the society of kind and friendly associates; and with them apparently enjoy seasons of pleasure and mirth; but amidst all of this, and in all of the finely furnished mansions and costly residences, if we are not greeted by the pleasant smiles; and familiar voices of Fathers, Mothers. Sisters and Brothers; what a vacancy their is around us, in the midst of crowds.

No place like home! Is the constant inward motto, which always prompts us, to seek after every source of conversation, which perhaps might for a time draw our thoughts from the past: and engage them in the surrounding amusements of the present.

But alas! In vain is our search, for the ties which bind in one common bond, the affections and thoughts of our hearts. with those who frequent the home of our youth are not to be severed by the cold, yet seemingly warm friends of pleasure.

Home is the dearest place on earth. It is there we first lisp the names of our parents; and by them are taught to repeat the sweet words of a Saviors love; and then to join in the song of thanks for daily blessings. It is there, in the begining of life, and with innocent prattle, that we are firmly linked in the chain of love with the affections of Brothers and Sisters.

When pleasantly seated around the hearth, with the circle complete, and all, either engaged in some interesting conversation, or in reading, in my estimation, there can be nothing added, that will increase the beauty of their certainly happy scene.

But let their circle be broken. After death has pronounced his sentence and clothed his victim, pale and icy, in the robes of the tomb; and wafted the spirit across the rolling billows: What a change has taken place in home, one pleasant face, smiling countenance, and familiar voice is forever hushed in silence.

The last gaze upon the marble brow is not

soon to be forgotten, as it calmly and sweetly lay sleeping.

The chain is again divided and another link is taken for the ranks of the Eternal World. Although, conscious of the wisdom of Providence such a blow can not be withstood without the shedding of many a silent tear, from the sense of being separated for a time, from those dearly loved.

And recalling past associations, as we vacantly stare at the empty seat, everything around is enstamped with solitude and mourning. Even the lamp which before burned brightly, seems now, but dim, scarcely shedding one ray of light to the eyes of those who are left behind.

It is now, nothing but a pale blaze, slowly flickering away, and this reminding us, that such must be in turn; our fate passing from our timely home to our Eternal rest.

WHAT HAST THOU GLEANED TO-DAY.

This is a very important question. Although, it consists of but five small words, and at first thought, many would say they are very insignificant in their meaning, and pass them by, with so saying; without thinking that it would do no harm to confer another thought, especialy on any sentence that contains the word to-day, which implies volumes, that may never be revealed, not because, to-morrow may never dawn, but should it, perhaps those who were to solve these unknown mysteries, may be called to give a final account of what they have gleaned during the time allotted to them for this purpose.

It is a question, that should be pondered often and well, by those who wish to attain some useful position, while in this state of probational life, as well as by those who are preparing themselves to inherit a higher, and more important station, the kingdom of God.

Ever against a great deal of apposition, each day, we should glean something from the wide field of intellectual and moral knowledge.

"Since little by little, great things are accomplished."

We may thus acquire a large store of that which is beautiful and useful: and also, gain mentally, great superiority over those who are waiting and expecting to receive suddenly and without any effort, these things, which to them will never come, as they can only be procured by patient and incessent labor.

Are we, a band of gleaners, as we profess to be, by meeting here from time to time, by having our names enrolled on the class-book of the several branches of study, and by our presence each day, thoroughly gleaning the ground over which we are passing?

And are we eagerly listening to. and grasping after that which is being dropped by our teachers; and for that which has been printed on the pages of our books, for our improvement, by those who have preceeded us? By many, these questions will be negatively answered.

How many can review their days, that were spent at school, and decide upon a single day of their school life, and recommend it as an example by which they would wish others to follow, but comparatively few of them, even the Professers and Teachers would be willing to comply with this.

There are those, though painful to reflect, who after canvassing the field of knowledge, and arriving too late, to amend at a period of reflection, recall many instances, in which they left whole sheaves unbroken and unnoticed; and many clusters, which are all still waving, as though the field had never been tread by the reapers.

They view this field with a wishful, and a longing eye; and with a heart full of regret, that they had entered; and passed along with such blindness; they are now perfectly surprised at their negligence of having left so much which was within their power to acquire.

What a satisfaction it would now be if they could reach back to childhood days; and from then to the present, make the corrections, which they now see could be made, in the meandering paths of life.

But time past can never be reclaimed; and the works performed therein can never be undone. Since fate has thus marked out our course, so must it remain.

This should be an instructive lesson, for those, in the future who have listened to the affecting story of those who have been thus disappointed at the close of their gleaning time, and it should prompt us to seek after the smallest particles, procure them and solve their worth.

That we may have a ready answer and a good report when we hear the question; What hast thou gleaned to-day?

"THY FATHER'S VIRTUE IS NOT THINE."

We as children undoubtedly look forward with delight to that time when we shall become by right the heirs of our father's possessions. And with particular eagerness do we await such an e-vent provided we know that our father is a just one; and that we are assured of receiving the por-tion due us; which will not be ours, because we have the decree to claim it; but because our father is willing and desirous of bestowing upon us these boons.

Although it be true that the father possesses this generous heart, and with it much to give. Although he is commander of armies, owner of tribes, and worthy of having all persons call him great; yet there is one gem, virtue, or his true worth which he cannot give to his child.

He who would be more than a blank in his neighbors estimation, and on memories pages, must be it by his own exertions. If he wishes others to say and know that he is living for an aim, that he is here to aid the the needy of the world, and to do what he can for the bettering of society, he must be in the possession of this jewel, which he can only obtain by his own toil, and which if duly cultivated will place him in the highest degree of elevation.

There is no vocation in life however simple that can be rightly filled by one who has no merit which he can claim as his, who will not dare to do as his concience dictates, and who has no principles of his own to put into use, but who must beg or steal the implements he needs. This may be done by the one in almost any kind of business, but his beggary or theft which ever it may be can be detected at once, by any person who can see anything.

It is plain that he who is sailing alone on the rough billows of the sea, drifted about upon its threatening waves must with a steady, and unceasing motion work his own oars, if he would reach the desired haven in safty. His father may be skilled in every principle that is needful concerning sea life, but not the least assistance can he give to his needy child. And just as the voyager allows it so shall the waters hurl him.

Each and all are sailing on an unfathomed and angry sea, called life: whose tide eager, is ever willing to bear portage down, down with its rapid current until it has conveyed it to a port of dispair, from whence there is no return.

Wherever our career on this unstable sea, whether drifted about from haven to haven, or carried by a smooth gale, if we would reach the anchorage for which we are aiming our ship must be rowed toward that place by our own labor; for should we trust another to do it for us, we would too frequently be found drifting in the direction of waves to an unknown place, and without a guide.

Some of us while toiling for an education may at times think that we are giving our money, our time, and some of us even our health, from which is derived the greatest enjoyment of life, without seeing much good result. Although to us it may so seem yet the one who takes as a rule justice to himself, and is not afraid to exercise his mental faculties, is laying the foundation for a character which no man can give or take away. But I must say it, not because it should be so, that there are persons who do not take this as their guide, and who for this manner of doing, are accustomed to construct numerous varieties of excuses, but none of them will pass a civil test.

Some of this class will say if I only had money, and a third part if I only had talent.

But what of these excuses, some of the most well doing and illustrious men that the world has known, have been those who had no friends until they won them by their worth, who had no money until they made it, and who had no talent until with labor they scoured from its surface the rustiness, and wrecked the sluggishness which clung to its material.

There certainly is no person who can find a true defence for his nonprogression. so long as he has health and reason, and if the first of these does not impede his advance. we must conclude that it is the latter which does.

No person has a just reason for thinking that there is nothing for him to do, because some person else can seemingly do more, or has had a better commencement and more assistance. For there are as many individuals of worth who have arisen from poverties home, yes more than those who have come from wealths abode.

Where do we generaly see the landing of that youth who has all the money he desires, and which he obtains in some other way than by his own labor. In his unthinking moments he may imagine that his fathers good name will secure for him friends and all things necessary for his enjoyment. But too soon do we find him an unlearned. unthinking man, in the lowest possession that degredation can place him. His father may be a true and devoted hero to all that is right and elevating. But alas his child in a place of horrid misery. in danger of eternal destruction, to which money and friends have borne him, and from which his own father cannot rescue him.

The fantasy is false that some persons are carried through life along flowery paths of ease. To the looker on these places may seemingly be joyous, while to those permeating them they comprise nothing of sunshine and happiness.

Although the picture of these might indicate to the observer that their lives were more cheerful than others, yet they are not even so much as acquainted with the joys of life, nor is their situation one to be desired. And should they trust to scenes like these for their portage through life, through life, they would never go.

And truly did the poet think when he said:

> Up this world, and down, this world,
> And over this world and through,
>   Though drifted about,
>   And tossed without,
>   We must row our own canoe.
>
> What though our sky is heavy with clouds,
>   Or shining a field of blue;
>   If the black wind blows,
>   Or the sunshine glows,
>   We must row our own canoe.
>
> There are daisies springing along the shores
>   Blooming and sweet for you;
>   There are rose-hued dyes
>   In the autumn skies,
>   If you row your own canoe.—Lou Zeller.

MUSICAL CONCERT.

You will find enclosed, as a quotation,
The topics of the song, by notation;
And in rhyme the idea will be conveyed,
Of sentiment, and of music made.

And should I fail in point of praise,
'Twill be in that I do not raise,
In words the impression on my heart,
Made by the strains of this concert,

A Sunday-school concert of singing
Was held at College the fifth of May,
Within its walls had ne'er such singing,
Been heard till the eve of this day.

When called to order, the school did sing
"O, we were youthful soldiers" if
To God, amidst all trouble, we cling;
While climbing from valley to cliff.

Then prayer by Rev. S. W. Zeller;
And to hear the pleading for right.
All listened as if in silent awe
They stood before their Maker's sight.

"If I come to Jesus," the infant class,
Next, sung in simple words, yet sweet:
As if they had come from angelic bliss,
With angel tongue, the song to repeat.

"Beautiful Sabbath," by clear and
young,
Soft voices, in strains that seem
blending
With the tunes made by spirit tongue,
On the breeze of eve was wending.

Then the school sung, O! what is loved
    best
  Of all the books moral or libel,
No fiction, verse or prose of just,
  But "God's blessed book the Bible."

"Reunion in Heaven," music did swell
  By classes combined, yet to sever,
In this reunion, joy will dispel,
  All sorrow of parting forever.

In pleasure or pain, labor or ease,
    A 'warning voice,' ever solemn im-
    parts,
The truth of two roads across the seas,
    And says, soft yet stern, prepare
    your hearts!"

President Allen a speech did give,
  Concerning the school, its aims and
    views,
He in words that will ever live,
  Of the truths that those absent shall
    lose!

A class of boys affirmed, in song,
  And in sweet notes the tune did glide
That to this earth Jesus looks down,
  And does His "little reapers" guide.

The "Harvest Home," by a quartette,
  Was like a vision before us brought;
Telling of the pleasure there, and yet
  To enjoy this home, we must be taught

The Lord commands us, ever and above,
  All else, to know that Jesus for us
Come to earth through pity and love,
  Then, Lord, "Remember Me," and
  keep me thus.

"A penny a day," we were informed,
  To those who labor would be given;

And many a star our crown will adorn
When we reach the shore called
Heaven.

Those most dear are "Going one by one'
Like the sand of the hour glass, slow
They have reached that land. their
journeys done,
Of either happiness or woe

In memory we cherish their names:
And long for the smiles of their face:
And familiar they come in our dreams,
Seeming still to be filling their place.

Who does not "Welcome Sabbath
morninig,"
With its rest from labor and toils!
And who would not greet each morn
returning,
That brings us balm to ease turmoil?

"Jusus Came," from his beautiful home
on high.
Down to this world of shame and sin,
And on the cross with thieves did die:
That Eternal life we might win.

Angels chant for the coming of others,
To their home; will they not when
we,
With parents and sisters and brothers
Together meet o'er "the crystal sea?"

Thirty-four voices in the last place
Swelled praises to their giver,
And told how music would never cease,
"When we cross the crystal river."

How instinctively nature presents to us at different times the changeable phases of man's real characters. The peculiar properties which belong to his disposition of heart, whether favorable to his separation, in general, or not, can easily be detected by the discriminating observers.

Sometimes, however, man by a long and careful training can exhibted to the eye of others an illusive appearance; and, with the aid of false airs, cause them to believe that such is his true and invariable temper, when, perhaps, beneath this quantity of cultivated deception lies hidden a heart as corrupt and depreaved as that of any of those vicious persons. who flood the streets of our cities and towns: and keep up the din and riot therein.

Although, such persons are skillful in some instances in governing, and controling their temper within due limits, for which they should certainly be commended, yet often, as soon as some trivial dispute concerning their interests, arises among those with whom they are associated; and, when the brittle thread which holds their irritable spirits is broken, they are around, in a twinkling, from their obscured chambers; into which, no doubt, they have repeatedly retreated sealing the doors, with the words, "You shall never again obtain possession of all the agreeable qualities of my nature."

But now being aroused; regardless of the elevation which they wished to obtain in the estimation of others. They are at once engaged in all manner of reproachful threats and improper language. And thus, with their passions enraged to the highest pitch, they are tossed hither and thither upon the rough billows of the stream of uncontrol.

Many persons while seeking happiness are already standing on the mountain of sunshine; and in the vally of gloom and dispair; and at each change from the mountains to the valleys, the inward phases are characterized, in a degree, by the peaceful, or, the restless and unquiet expression either brightness or overshadows the countenance.

Men do not always need a written recommenda-
tion or condemnation to secure them an acceptance, or a rejection, either in respect to a position
in business, or the favor of others; for the inscrip-
tion of the ruling motive is plainly enstamped upon their every feature and every deed performed
in society.

There is, truly speaking, no path in this world,
that can guarentee safety to the deceptious individual, who, endeavors to gain the victory; and
still cherish the inward foe; and without observ-
ing the inconsistancy in attempting to present
before the world a fictitious sembiance of virtue,
they persist in this course. Meanwhile, they do
not obtain much credit with others for their vain
efforts, for through this filmy curtains, the true
picture can be viewed, as it is painted upon the
reflecting walls of the soul.

The most desirable path, among the different
varieties, that are placed before our judgement,
from which we can continually conduct our hearts
and actions, as will be in harmony with Divine
Providence.

Then the appearances of the inner life can not
vary to any distinguishable extent either at morn-

ing, noon, or night, as the interior principles are fully portrayed by the exterior, through the means of our words and actions.

Let the heavy crushing weight of disappointment of some contemplated future enjoyment or pleasure, fall upon the innocent heart of that sunny-faced youth; and what remarkable change occurs in the expression of the eye and in the tones of the voice! And, often, a consoling word or a kind look of sympathy is but a thorn piercing deeper than ever into the afflicted feelings; arousing afresh the faithful thoughts of the present gloom, and vividly bringing up the vision of the might have been pleasant realities.

Then let one ray of sunshine be admitted to the troubled heart, with the tidings that the disappointment is false; and what will be the result? In a moment an expression of joy accompanied by streakings of sunlight will be creeping over the brow, and will fill the heart with unutterable delight; and the gloom may be seen slowly passing away from its impatient companion.

Ever, then, before the imagination should we keep upon spangled canvas, in gilded letters, a motto, "Guard well your passions, for the want of

the soul's chamber is almost absolutly transpar-
ent; and being thus, are unveiled to the view of
others the phases of the inner life."

"MENTAL BEAUTY."

The only true mode of determining the beauty
of the mind is from its intrinsic qualities. By a
knowledge of its real worth, its skill, and its fit-
ness for the various departments of work in the
field in which it labors, are we furnished with the
key to the beautiful and pleasing chambers of
the soul.

All this cannot be perceived by the eye at first
view. The eye must carefully follow for a time
the quiet workings of nature as she is successively
exhibiting her grace that are pecular to the opera-
tions of the mind.

It is true that nature displays magnificence and
splendor in all her structures. There is a perfect
harmony of parts in the plan of natural things
throughout the entire universe. Of course there

is that which excites our feelings of admiration and wonder in the arrangement of the luminous bodies in the ethereal heavens. Also, in the systematic order of continents, oceans, islands, lakes, mountains, plains and valleys, on this our own sphere.

But do we not recognize a more beautiful supply of the beautiful and sublime in this one of her departments, the mind, than in any other? Does nature not here find the efficiency and scope to produce her brilliant effects, in a greater degree than elswhere? Most certainly she does! The soul can not now comprehend nor the imagination conceive of the vastness of present discoveries in mental glories; and the field is still being explored and extended in both breadth and depth. As we review the past and survey the present, what do we see? We learn that there is now in the intellectual meadows much more that receives our admiration and praise, than existed one hundred years ago. And we dare not say that the amount will not bedoubled or even quadrupled at the period of 1973.

We can scarcely calm our passions from becoming envious of that mind, of its gift of genius.

Who has invented and assembled the many minute machines into one grand combination, for the purpose of facilitating labor; for that of delighting the eye or for pleasing the ear.

We can see the beauty of the mind and estimate its real worth, only as we ourselves are prepared for this purpose. Our own minds must be cultivated in order that we may enjoy the education of others.

He that is wholly ignorant of science and knowledge in general, can not duly appreciate the products of minds well versed in the same. He can find but little pleasure and derive less benefit from hearing an address from one of the classics. "Why is this?" You may ask. Simply because his mental faculties are not sufficiently strong to digest that which is so well matured.

As the mind grows and advances in science, it will seek its food in that field; but he whose mind is not being cultivated seemingly desires no better food than the lowest and most vulgar expressions, language, and thoughts.

Almost universally the mind seeks for its companions among its equals. The one class searches for the society of the educated and refined; while the others look around for that of the rude and illiterate. To these last the mind "is without form or comeliness that they should desire it."

But after all, may not the beauty of every thing be said to exist in the mind? When we admire an object; and call it beautiful, may it not be the simple echo of our feelings; the reflection of the emotions that are within us upon some outward object? It may be from certain feelings of piety and love, or from some other affections that we may possess for the object so called beautiful. For the same object others may regard in an entirely different manner.

The more that is to be admired we have in our own possession the more we will see in others. God is the beautiful of all beauties.

It is He alone that can satisfy our inward longings. He is the lovliest object of the heart, and the most ravishing of the imagination. With Him as our pattern we can acquire and store within us much that will secure a life of happiness for ourselves, and also for those around us.

THERE'S PLENTY OF ROOM UP STAIRS.

Up to the chambers of knowing,
Numbered with Learning's blest heirs.
A band of sisters were going,
For there's plenty of room up stairs.

We're strewing sweet roses along
The pathway of those who are players;
And ask them to join in our song,
As we go to the room up stairs.

E'en the poor child of dependence
Can come and go up, if he dares,
For there's food for the mind in abundance
And there's plenty of room up stairs.

This world contains a giddy throng,
A certain class of people; who
With no fixed motive, pass along,
Regardless of the good and true.

With pleasure as their constant guide
They're drifted o'er the stream of time;
And on the surface, with the tide,
Forget there is an upper clime.

"Oh! days go by in swift reduction,"
They shrilly cry: and, plunging ott,
Go down the sea of dire destruction,
With total loss of all aloft.

They miss as often as they obtain
The object of their strong desire,
For pleasure they can't long retain;
And know not of an object higher.

Their minds by every simple tale
Are quickly aroused and swiftly tossed,
As a tiny boat by rushing gale
Is roughly whirled and likely lost.

Bedazzled by some gaudy treasure,
Not half do scan life's ocean wide,
But, with heart brimful of pleasure,
Soon they're drifting with the tide.

Oh! that all would choose to leave
The room below, and all its wares;
And from to-night begin to wear
Their thoughts with those who dwell up-
    stairs.

For harmony is found to dwell,
Where all demean themselyes like broth-
    ers—
Forever found promoting well,
The great design: Good will to others.

And each will then be fitting still,
His mind and heart for endless life;
And when we constant do God's will,
There's all of love, and naught of strife.

Then sorrow's moan shall cease its ringing,
In that blithest place where none have
    cares,
Where every heart breaks forth in sing-
    ing.
In heaven's unbounded room upstairs.

IN MEMORIAM.

WHEREAS, It hath seemed good in the wisdom and love of our ever kind Father to again send the messenger of Death into the Philalethean Literary Society of Westfield College, and take from our little band still another one of its most faithful, honored and dearly beloved members, Miss S. Angie Zeller, of Westfield, Ill., and

WHEREAS, We deem it fitting that we give public expression to our sorrow and our sense of irreparable loss in the death of our dear sister; therefore,

RESOLVED: That in this sad and unexpected dispensation we behold the work of the Divine hand, and desire humbly to bow in submission and say, "Thy will is done." That we truly feel that our hearts are closely united in sympathy with those of the stricken family and we would tenderly mingle our tears with theirs in this the hour of their sore affliction, when their wounded hearts are made to bleed afresh under this, the second stroke; yet remembering that "Whom He loveth He chasteneth," and believing that on the other shore a happy band is forming, composed of those who are passing over, never again to be separated.

RESOLVED: That we will ever cherish fondly and sacredly her memory, around which cluster so many sweet associations, and strive day by day to follow in the footsteps of the blessed Redeemer, whom she so loved and who sustained her in her dying hour.

BIOGRAPHY.

LOUISA ANN ZELLER,

The third in age, was born in Westerville, Franklin county, Ohio, February 10, 1855. She was very hearty and robust from her earliest infancy. And on account of her sound physical constitution, she was what mothers call a good child. While quite young she would eat and sleep and hardly ever cry, She grew very rapidly and was soon a fine, interesting girl. Nothing of any note occurred until she was about the age of five years. She soon learned the alphabet and was noted for her ability to spell correctly. Before she could read she won the prize in her class for spelling. For three consecutive terms after this, she bore away the prize in triumph, being the best speller of her class. She was a very hearty girl, and I think very few persons have passed through life with less affliction than she did, at least this is true up to within two weeks before her death.

She had good privileges and advantages in in-
telectual and moral culture until we left Wester
ville, which occured when she was ten .years of
age. She attended Sabbath-school and the other
means of grace in the vicinity of our new home,
where we remained a little over two years. She
gave no evidence of any special interest in the
christian religion until two months after she was
twelve years of age, when she was awakened and
happily converted under very remarkable circumstances. In the Spring of the year 1867, we moved
four miles west of the city of Lancaster, Ohio, on
the circuit I was then traveling. We arrived at
our new home the day she was twelve years and
two months old. We were part of two days making the journey of a little over forty miles. Having completed the trip at four o'clock on the second day, and the kind friends who were soon to
be our associates having cleaned the house and
made it ready for us to occupy. The two teamsters
who assisted me to move, and myself, were soon
busily engaged in unloading the wagons, aud fix-
ng up things generally for a nights lodging. Her
brother, nearly nine years old, came to where I
was unloading a wagon, and said, with tears in his

eyes, said to me: "Louisa wants you to come in and pray for her. She says she is going to die." I immediately stopped my work, and went to the house and inquired of her mother what was wrong with the girl. She replied; "She is awakened and troubled with convictions for sin." She had gone upstairs. I went up and found her in the farthest room back in the house, all alone sighing and weeping. I inquired what was the cause of her sadness: "O," said she, "I am such a great sinner, I know not what to do." This was the first intimation I had that such sadness and gloom were weighing her down. Her mother, however, has noticed for some time that she was more than ordinarily sad, and troubled with a meloncholy state of mind. I was at home but a short time, and was very busy in getting ready to move; this will in part account for my entire ignorance of her condition. Some of the members of the family had already carried a number of the articles of household furniture upstairs, and also some books among which was a volume of the New Testament and Psalms. I suppose; indeed, that she had been assisting the rest of the family in this work until she broke down with grief and sorrow.

.I spoke a few words of encouragement to her, and then seeing this Book of God near, I picked it up and turned to the sermon of Jesus on the Mountain; and told her to read it carefully and ask the Savior anxiously in prayer ;and to trust in him with all her heart; and she would find peace in his pardoning love.O, how thankful we ought to be to our Father in Heaven for the cheering and comforting promises of His Holy Word. Although she was only a little over twelve years of age, she could read quite well, and this was a great help to her in seeking the Savior. I then went back to my work, for it was then nearly night, and no arrangements consummated for eating and sleeping; and she had to struggle with her sorrows as best she could during the night. By diligence and activity, we soon succeeded in getting the wagons unloaded and things in the house. We then had some victuals prepared to satisfy the demands of nature, and then we kneeled down and asked God's blessings upon us, and protection over us during the night. The morning light came, but no peace to Louisa's mind. We again knelt around the family alter in prayer, reserving the more complete dedication of the house in which we expected to live for a time to a future day, as

as it afterwards turned out. After spending a little
time in convsrsation with her on the subject of
religion, and encouraging her to trust in the blessed Jesus, I went to get a cow we left on the way,
twelve miles back; this required the whole day,
and it was night when I returned. During this
day and the following night she was exceedingly
sad and heart broken. The next day being the
second after we moved, after attending to some
work somewhat pressing, I determined to have a
prayer meeting in our new home. I said to Louisa:
Would you like for us to have a prayer meeting?
It may be a blessing to you." I shall never forget her reply "I am willing for anything that will
bring me relief." We then went into the back
room, the farthest from the road, and commenced
devotional exercises. There were three of us who
professed religion at the meeting, Mrs. Zeller,
Miss Angie and myself. Mary E., the oldest, of
whom I have written, was not at home, and several other children. We joined in singing and then
I led in yrayer; then, after the singing, her mother led in prayer. I encouraged her to pray, and
at once she looked to Jesus for salvation. By this
time she had become very much in earnest, pray-

ing and pleading faithfully for the blessing of
saving grace. And, indeed, we were having rather
a stirring time. There was a family living near
us who would hear the singing and praying, and
the plaintive cries of the penitent; so I sent the
little boy to their home to tell them that we were
holding religious services at our house, and that
they should come and attend the meeting, but
they were not enjoying all the religion it was their
privilege to enjoy, for when I called on them to
sing they could not. I did not mean that they
had no musical tallent, but to sing at this meeting
under such circumstances was not at all congenial
with their feelings. One of them said to me; "Shall
I go and get Uncle Benjamin to help at the meeting? He is a good hand at these meetings." I
replied that she might if she wished; so she started
out for her uncle and her sister followed her, but
neither of them returned to the meeting. Their
uncle was the class leader at that place, and was
an active, faithful christian. We kept on singing
and praying, for we had much to encourage us,
for Jesus said: "Where two or three are gathered
together in my name, there am I in their midst,"
and so it was, for He was with us in converting

power; in a moment her sin ▪ ▪ ▪ ▪ ▪ she was happy in the love of Jesus. Her gloom and sorrow were all gone, and peace, and love reigned in her soul. A few moments after her conversion. Uncle Benjamin, the leader, came in. I said to him: You have come too late to the meeting. It has closed. "It is all right," said he, "I am glad it has closed so well." He stayed some time. and held an interesting conversation with her who had just entered upon the new life of faith in Jesus. She enjoyed herself very much in the religion of our Lord Jesus Christ, and went forward in the duties of a religious life with more than ordinary freedom and delight.

In the fall of the year after she was fourteen years of age, she entered the Union School of Lancaster, Ohio, where she had good opportunities for mental culture for nearly three years; and here she made rapid advancement in her studies When a little past seventeen she entered the College at Westfield,, Clark Co., Ill. She was as distinguished for her industry and success in college as she had proven herself to be in the primary department of education

She would not be behind any one of her class, and if she could excel she was all the better satisfied. She was a Sabbath school teacher the last year of her life, and sustained this relation when she died. She assisted in taking care of her two sisters during their sickness, and saw both of them buried. She then commenced showing indications of an attack of the same fever, and I became much concerned about her welfare. I secured a good physician to undertake her case, who had ten days the start of the fever, but with all this advantage, his efforts and skill failed to arrest the disease, and when the attack was made it terminated fatally with her.

There was a good deal of excitement in our town with refrence to this disease, some thought it was caused by one thing, and some thought by an other. Some thought the poison was in the air, while others were of the opinion that the disease could be traced to local causes; but it was dificult to decide this matter definitely, and to this day it is still a mistery. I think it is quite doubtful if the cause will ever be known.

Some days before she was

taken with the fever I was expressing my fears of the result. She spoke to us very decidedly, and said: "It will be all right, let it terminate as it will. If it is the will of the Lord that I should die, it is all right, and if it is His will that I should get well it will be all right. Now do not censure yourselves about any thing you may think was not attended to right, and do not think you made a mistake here and a mistake there." She appeared to be entirely resigned to the will of God. My fears were fully realized. She had such a malignant attack of the fever that it resulted in her death in about twelve days.

I never knew a case of fever that raged with such unabated fury. The physicians could do nothing with it. The pulse beat as rapidly as it possibly could in a human being; not less than 140 beats to the minute during the last two or three days of her life. The physical system undergoing such a wonderful strain would soon wear out.

About two days before she died she requested me to sing that interesting piece of music called "The Home of the Soul," I made the effort, and she joined in a full, loud voice and assisted me to sing. She became more calm and rational the

day before she died, and talked very beautifully a-
bout her prospects of a home in the better land
in Heaven, where sickness and sorrow, pain and
death will be felt and feared no more forever. She
bid adieu to the scenes of this life with its suffering and troubles about two o'clock on the 7th of
October, 1873. The funeral services were conducted by Rev. H. Elwell and Pres. S. B. Allen
before a large congregation in the College Chapel,
and then her remains were laid beside her sisters
who had so recently left us and gone before her.

The next day after she was buried, Laura, the
only girl we then had living, about twelve years
of age, was taken sick very much as the others
were. We sent her with a friend to the circuit
that I received as my field of labor at a recent session of the Conference, held during our siege of affliction. The following day the rest of us, con-
sisting of my companion, a little boy and myself,
started for my new field of labor; we arrived there
on the second day, and found the girl very sick
indeed, it was quite an undertaking for one not
well, to travel so far in one day in a private conveyance. Now we were called upon once more
watch over and take care of another sick child, a

work that over a month of constant watching,
care and anxiety had made quite familiar to us.
She lay dangerously ill for two weeks; part of this
time we had serious doubts of her recovery; but in
the kind Providence of God her life was spared,
and she was permitted to remain with us for our
cheer and comfort; and she soon recovered her usual health again. We returned home after an absence of nearly a month to realize the sad loss as
only those can realize who have passed through
similar scenes of bereavement.

THE READER WILL NOW BE FAVORED WITH
SOME OF LOUISA'S WRITINGS.

"CIVILIZATION."

In this country it is the privilege of evry person
whether rich or poor, whether they belong to this
class of persons or to that, to be advanced to some
degree in civilization.

The time has been when civilization was unknown in this part of the globe. When this country called America was only known by the bar-

barous and savage tribes. who supported life by
fishing and hunting; and whose greatest enjoyment consisted in roving through the forests.
They were created beings similar to those who
now occupy their places, and yet how different
were their lives. They were not capable of rea-
soning, and they saw but little, if any beauty in
the things of nature or things around them; and
were almost entirely ignorant of themselves. They
know that they had a being. and but little else,
they knew not why or for what they were living,
nor could they solve the least mystery in the case
of a dying friend. They were unconcious of being in the possession of souls, and of all being the
children of one common Father. But since
their time what a change civilization has effected.
This country has arisen from a barbarous and
miserable condition, to one which is worthy of the
highest parise. Instead of the uncultivated fields
and forests, there are the well attended and productive farms, and the Commercial, Agricultural,
and other citties of importance.

Instead of their rude huts and wigwams, made
of undressed logs and trash of the woods, there

are the beautiful and accommodating dwelling houses.

And where they would worship a string of beeds or something else as trifling in our eyes, we wor-. ship the true and living Lord.

We may look back and say wretched was their condition, and so it was. But in this day of enlightenment there are cases continually being brought before us, that are equally as wretched and pitiable as was theirs, and many that are far worse.

We are not justifiable in saying that if these persons in ancient times could live without any more labor and cultivation of mind than they did, that we can live in the same manner, for it is said in the Divine word that, "He to whom much is given of him much shall be required." I understand this to mean that he who has many privileges and talents shall be required to encrease his possession in proportion to the one who has less. We say that our country at the present time is a civilized one, but this does not imply that all of its inhabitants are civilized, although it should imply this, and great is the disgrace of those who are not of this class, and all of their excuses for doing wrong summed up together are as but trifles. For they have been shown right from wrong, they know it, and are earnestly laboring that they may not be lost.

What I understand by a civilized person is one who is refined in his habbits and manners, and who is to some degree acquainted with the arts and sciences, but we need not search long nor far to find persons who claim to be civilized, and yet, they possess more of these qualities. We may take for our example the drunkard, whose chief delight and comfort consists in satisfying his raging appetite with strong liquors, which are unfit for a civilized person to taste, such persons as these ought not to be regarded above the brute in civilization, nor even equal, for out of human beings whom God has given talent and mind, they are making persons equal to barbarians and beasts, yet these persons think that they are civilized and ought to be regarded as such. For another example we may take the wicked villain, who has never thought of being any one except a civilized person, he will in the darkness of the night force his way into and innocent neighbors house, and take his life in order that he may have in his possession a few dollars, which he regards as being a valuable treasure, but which is the means not only of destroying his character and life, but which is also preparing a dungeon of the deepest wretchedness for the dwelling of his immortal soul in the future. I cannot conceive of a world which such persons as these are worthy of having, and I think uncivilzed is too good. At the present age the greater part of mankind have attained to some degree in civilization, yet there is much room for improvement. Some have succeeded better than others, because they have labored more earnestly for the accomplishment of this end.

LIFE'S STREAM.

The stream on which we glide,
 May now have a smooth tide;
Our sky may be clear
 And all on earth most dear.

We may think we will always glide
 Along on the unruffled tide,
And that all of life so wide,
 Will calmly meet our side.

It may seem that trouble's rage,
 Shall never with us engage;
And bury our hopes of life
 Beneath the darkest night.

But sorrows will come at last,
  Though we saw it not in the past,
And in parts to us unknown
  We may wander all alone.

With not a friend below,
  To whom we may show,
The darkness of our day,
  And the scenes along the way.

But although this be our way,
  Let it not be to us forgot,
That above is a friend in need,
  Who will prove a friend indeed.

VOYAGE OF LIFE.

We are all voyaging o'er life's ocean,
  If sometimes the way seems dark,
Let us not give way to fashion,
  But onward push our bark.

Though we often meet in darkness,
  Let us think that help is near;
And always look for higher goodness,
  But never aside for fear.

In this battle we are sisters, one
  Not rebels against each other;
Then let us cheerfully work on,
  As a true brother would for a brother.

We are all fighting the same fight,
  The same victory we would gain;
We are climbing the same hight,
  And each linked in the same chain.

Why can't we all be firmly bound,
  By the same rich cord of love,
And then press on, hand in hand;
  'Till we reach the golden grove.

We were made to bear another's care,
   And to join in anothers grief,
If this be done our sky is fair,
   And peaceful shall be our death.

The same one has account of our deeds,
   He sees the frail webs we have woven,
And at God's right hand He faithfully
     pleads,
   That we all may be forgiven.

MAKING PIES.

On the thirtieth of August,
   In eighteen hundred, seventy-three,
My mother said: "now daughter Lou,
   Pies must be made by thee."

This was the day before Sunday,
   And sisters two I had,
The typhoid fever them had chained,
   Oh! they were very bad.

And all I knew was work, work, work,
   From early until late,
Nor had a soul revealed to me,
   The sorrow of my fate.

Mother, the command had given,
   Then to the sick she spake,
And she did'nt even tell me
   What kind of pies to make.

As I stood a moment, thinking
   What would be best to do,
I happened to see a pumpkin,
   Which was full ripe I knew.

I prepared it first for cooking,
   Then with the bucket went,
To the barn-yard in haste and hurry;
   For all the milk was spent.

Now our cows were very gentle,
  And good as they could be,
And surely they always were glad
  When me they once would see.

So I dreamed not of danger here,
  But friendly met the cow,
Who gave me such an awful kick
  That I just wondered how,

A brute that I had always loved,
  Could do me such a sin;
She laid me low, but I arose
  Without a single grin.

I did not say a word to those,
  Who now in sight looked on,
But to myself I deeply cried,
  Oh! has she broke my crown.

And as the blood did freely flow,
  My heels the faster sped,
To see if I was really hurt
  And had to go to bed.

A student gent was passing by,
  And thinking something wrong,
Stood still and with the kindest words,
  Asked the story or song.

My bucket lay beside the cow,
  While she contented seemed,
And thought I did not want to milk.
  But she had only dreamed.

Because in haste I left her there,
  And soon was out of sight;
No doubt she thought when I was gone,
  I've shown to her my spite.

The cow was thinking she had ruled.
  But ah! alas! in vain,
The gent who saw the act, milked her,
  And then returned the pain.

I went to bed and wet my head,
  For bruised was I indeed,
And now, for once in many years,
  I was a child in need.

NIGHT.

Beautiful night whose scenes we love,
  Is a gift from our God above;
Telling his children here on earth,
  To trust with Him their all of worth.

'Tis in darkness when we alone,
  Can truly feel our neighbor's moan,
And bended low in humble prayer,
  Tell our Father for them we care.

Each clings to something he loves best,
  And holds it above all the rest,
On this his joy of life depends,
  As onward to the grave he tends.

Not the world can his treasure buy,
  Nor will he tell the reason why,
Lest they should deem it no excuse,
  And in return himself abuse.

But give me right with its many charms
  When disapeared have all alarms;
No other time I'll place above,
  This sacred one of trust and love.

IN MEMORIAM.

Whereas, Our Father has seen fit, yet once more, to send mourning and sorrow into the Philalethean Society of Westfield College' by sending his messenger, Death, to bear away still another one of its brightest ornaments, a faithful and devoted member, Miss Lou A. Zeller, of Westfield, Illinois; and, *Whereas*, We, as sisters, desire to publicly express our deep sorrow and our sense of irreparable loss in the death of this dear one; therefore,

Resolved, 1. That in this, to us, mysterious and sad dispensation, we will endeavor to be submissive to the divine will; that we deeply sympathize with the afflicted family in this third sad stroke, and would tenderly mingle our tears with theirs in this hour of sorrow and grief,—yet trusting that they will look heavenward to the "many mansions" where their loved ones are going one by one, where broken links in the chain of affection shall be reunited, and where there will be no more death.

2. That we will ever hold in remembrance her noble character, endeared to us by so many sweet associations, and will endeavor to trust more and more in the dear Jesus who guided her footsteps in life, and who enabled her to sing his praises in her dying hour.

3. That we wear the usual badge of mourning thirty days

4. That a copy of these resolutions be presented to the family, and that they be recorded in the journal of our society, and that copies be sent for publication to the *Reigious Teescope, Clark County Herad, Marsha Messenger, Chareston Puindeaer, Ohio Eage*, and the *Westervie Banner*.

ETTIE PARCEL,)
DORA BOLTON, } Com.
MATTIE DAVES.)

Philalethian Hall, Oct. 7, 1873.

Daniel Oscar Zeller was born in Delaware Co. Ohio the 5 of Oct. 1868, about one mile north of the village of Westerville Delaware Co Ohio.

He had one brother older than himself, who died when only four months of age. He had three sisters who were older, whose biographies the reader has already been made familliar with. There is one brother and one sister who is still living. D. Oscar being the only boy in the family for some time, he was much thougt of. He was the favorite of the preachers who stoped with his father. He committed to memory a little speech that he would often repeat, and call it preaching. Ou one occasion O. S. a minister who often put up with the family, called him his little preacher. He said to the minister that he could preach,"Well then get up on a chair and preach." He at once mounted a chair and declaimed his speech. Rev. O. S. then gave him a dime and remarked that preachers who delivered sermons should be paid for their work.

He was about four years old when this o cured.

His mother heard him talking very pityingly one day to a calf that was in the yard, and saying to it "don't cry poor calfy, don't cry calfy." His mother ascertained by going to where he was that he had hit the calf with the sharp end of an ax, blood running from the wound frightened him badly: hence his effort to console the calf.

When he was about four years of age, his father was drafted to go into the army during the great rebellion, and this was rather a serious time with all the members of the family.

The government permitted those who were drafted to remain at home exempt from military duty by paying three hundred dollars. But the hard part of it was, in the early part of the war money was exceedingly scarce. Efforts were made to obtain the money, but it was a failure. The matter was talked over in the family; and it looked very much as if the father would have to bid adieu to the wife and children, and go out in defence of his country. My companion thought this could not be, but there was only one course to take if the money was not secured, and that was to bear arms in defence of our country, and it seemed impossible to get money at this time. Daniel Oscar was listening with intense interest at all that was said, and impressively remarked "Pa can't you pay out with eggs." The little fellow knew that his mother obtained a number of articles from the store with eggs, and thought this amount could be obtained in the same way. In the spring of 1865 the family moved about 26 miles, and he assisted in driving the stock to the new home. He was a very stirring and obedient boy. While the family lived in the city of Lancaster Ohio, he embraced religion at a meeting held in the M. E. Church, when only a little past twelve years of age. He said one day to his mother, during the the progress of the meeting that he thought he ought to make an effort to be religious. His mother did not think him sincere for he was quite jocular at times. On the next evening he was forward with other anxious penitents to the altar of prayer, and continued to go. time after time until he professed faith in the Lord Jesus. This was all voluntary upon his part, without persuasion from any one. He joined the church and attended the prayer and class meetings faithfully while he remained in the city.

In the summer of 1871 he went with the rest

of the family to Westfield Ill. He went to College during the fall, and winter of 1871 and 2. This was a very cold winter, and he took down with the typhoid pneumonia, which terminated fatally with him in less than one week. On Friday night before he was taken down with disease, he led in family prayer, and he had unusual liberty in devotion.

His father left home the next morning for his field of labor, and saw him no more until called home to see him on a bed of death. After traveling seventy miles, the writer was permitted to return home late at night, and be with him a few hours before his death. He suffered much during the night and next day; and on Saturday night, he bid adieu to a world of trouble, and has doubtless gone in dwell in the better land.

DANIEL OSCAR ZELLER, son of Rev. S. W and Mary G. Zeller, died Feb. 18th, 1872, in the 14th year of his age. Rev. S. W. Zeller is a member of the Sciota Annual Conferance, but at present is a resident of Westfield, Illinois. His son, the subject of this notice, at the time of his death, was a student in Westfield College. A short time before he became religious, speaking upon the subject, he said, "Mother I have made up my mind to be a christtan." His religion sustained him through his short pilgrimage, and afforded him special consolation during his affliction. He said to his pastor, "I am ready to live or die. Jesus is precious! I am happy." And thus he calmly passed away. May God bless the bereaved parents and friends, and enable them to so live that they may meet their dear loved one in the paradise of God.   H. Elwell.

IN MEMORIAN.

WHEREAS, Our almighty Father, the author and dispenser of life, in the wisdom of his mysterious though righteous providence, has seen fit to cause the Zetagathean Literary Society, of Westfield College, to mourn the death of Oscar Zeller, of Westfield, Illinois, one of its most active and worthy members, as well as one of its most devoted and untiring friends.

WHEREAS, We feel called upon to give a public expression of our grief and consciousness of irreparable loss in the removal of our much-beloved brother; therefore,

Resolved, That in this bereavement we recognize the hand of our heavenly Father, and that we will meekly bow in submission, and say, "Thy will be done."

Resolved, That we truly sympathize with the bereaved family, and fain would mingle our tears with theirs in the bereavement they sustain, trusting that He who governs all things well may comfort and cheer them with his love in this hour of sadness, and that the loved bond, so suddenly severed here, may be re-united in the glory-world; where it shall never be broken,

Resolved, That we will endeavor to treasure up in our hearts a memory fraught with so many pleasant remembrances, and also to practice daily the precepts of the blessed religion in which faith he lived and died.

Resolved, That we wear the usual badge of mourning for thirty days, and that our hall be draped in mourning the remainder of the college year.

Resolved, That a copy of these resolutions be presented to the afflicted family, and that a copy of them be spread on the journal of the society, and also, that copies be furnished for publication in the RELIGIOUS TELESCOPE, *Lancaster Gazette, Ohio Eagle,* CLARK COUNTY HERALD, CHARLESTON PLAINDEALER.,

G. THOMPSON, ⎫
M. R. BAIR, ⎬ Com.
L. S. TOHILL, ⎪
E. R. SMITH ⎭